C000174650

Kintsugi

JUDE LENNON

Kintsugi

First published in 2022

Copyright 2022 Jude Lennon

All rights reserved.

ISBN: 978-1-915083-02-9

Cover design by Michelle Catanach

No part of this book may be reproduced
(including photocopying or storing in any medium
by electronic means and whether or not
transiently or incidentally to some other use of
this publication) without the written permission
of the copyright holder except in accordance
with the provisions of the Copyright, design
and patents Act 1988.

This book is a work of fiction. Names, characters,
businesses, organisations, places and events other
than those clearly in the public domain, are either the
product of the author's imagination or are used
fictitiously. Any resemblance to actual persons, living
or dead, events or locales is entirely coincidental.

Independently published with the support of
TAUK Publishing

DEDICATION

For Dom, who encourages me to follow my creative dreams –
always.

PROLOGUE

15th May 1968

As soon as I saw my mother, I knew there was something wrong. Her normally smiling face looked positively drawn.

When she walked into the room, I could feel the nervous tension she brought with her. Immaculately dressed, as usual, her beautiful clothes were a thin disguise. Her posture, normally so upright, was aged and weary, and she made her way hesitantly across the room towards me. With shaking hands, she reached out and clasped mine before guiding me to the settee. Once we were seated, she seemed uncertain how to continue. The seconds passed, and with a ragged breath, she released my hands only to clasp and wring her own until I couldn't bear it any longer and laid mine over hers to still them.

"What's the matter, Mum? Is it Dad? Or Grandma?" A knot of fear formed in my stomach.

"Your father's coming now. We need to tell you together."

Now thoroughly alarmed, I raised my eyes to the doorway as my father appeared. The smile he usually reserved for his daughters was missing and he took up position by the fireplace. He looked so remote; I almost didn't recognise him. What on earth could be the matter?

"Please, just tell me," I begged. "You're really scaring me." My mother cleared her throat and I waited for the blow.

"Your father and I, well... er...actually, not your father and I... I'm sorry, darling, I'm making an awful mess of this. It's so terribly difficult."

As always, in times of stress, she placed her whole dependence on my father, who once more stepped in to save her. His usually calm voice trembled, but the words were finally free and clear.

"We love you so very much. We always have, and we always will, but the truth is, although we have loved you as ours, you aren't actually ours. Your mother and I aren't your parents."

Time stood still, but the clock on the fireplace ticked on. Surely I'd misheard? My breath caught in my chest and the walls closed in around me. If I hadn't been sitting, I swear I would have fallen to the floor. I was stunned. My father's words had made sense when they left his mouth, but the air all around had tangled them into something utterly incomprehensible.

2

"What do you mean?" I whispered.

"We aren't your real parents, darling." My mother's tears fell freely. They splashed onto her dress, leaving stains and blemishes. "Please believe us, Eve. This changes nothing, sweetheart. We still love you wholeheartedly." Her hands were clutching mine so tightly my fingers were crushed.

I pulled them free and stood up. My legs felt strangely detached from my body, but they made the shaking steps across the room to the window. I gazed out onto the idyllic garden where I'd celebrated my twenty-first birthday just two months previously. My gaze wandered to the apple tree at the far end, which was still home to the swing drifting in the breeze. A garden full of childhood memories with my sister, Susan. Or not my sister as it now transpired. In one sentence, I had been bereft of Mum, Dad and sister. I was an orphan, cast out on the world. I leaned my head against the glass, and although it cooled my forehead, there was no comfort.

Helen and Francis Fenwick were not my parents. Mum and Dad were not my mum and dad. My sister was not my sister. The phrases repeated themselves around and around. Eventually, my brain accepted the words and tried to process what they meant.

I turned to face them. Francis had joined Helen on the settee and she was weeping freely into his shoulder. They looked broken.

"So, if *you* aren't my parents...?"

CHAPTER 1

2019

It had started like any typical Friday. I'd been to my regular 'Leisurely Ladies' Zumba' class and was showered and ready for the day ahead.

First things first, of course—tea. I hummed as the kettle boiled on the old Aga; its cosy warmth filled the kitchen like a comforting hug. The Aga had been a strictly practical thing when we had moved in all those years ago. There had been nothing glamorous about its ability to heat the house and provide hot water, but something had told us to keep hold of it even when we renovated. Now, of course, they are the height of new kitchen chic. Our neighbours had offered us a generous amount of money if we'd wanted to sell ours. We hadn't, and I couldn't imagine a time when we ever would. It was part of the house, just as Clive and I were.

It was a beautiful morning and the sun shone brightly enough to lift the spirits of anyone. I glanced out of the window onto our good-sized garden with trees, shrubs and flowers of all colours. Over in the corner, just touching the branches of the cherry tree, was the Summer House. I know this sounds ridiculous as it's only a building, but just looking at it always made me smile.

I'd wanted one for years, and Clive had surprised me for my thirtieth birthday. The planning and subterfuge required to get it done in secret had been worthy of MI5. My parents had ably assisted with childcare, and my sister Susan, and her husband Duncan, had 'suggested' a birthday weekend away, which Clive and I had snapped at. When we returned home, Clive had told me 'no peeping' before guiding my steps through the house and out into the garden. My eyes had widened in wonder when they were finally allowed to take in this most perfect gift. It was beautifully made and beautifully given.

Octagonal and constructed from cedar wood, it was my little sanctuary. I'd decorated it with care and had optimistically filled it with a chaise longue and bookcase before the weather of the Scottish Borders reminded me that I'd need to be a little more practical. More appropriate wicker furniture with removable cushions and a sturdy table had been shipped in as replacements and they'd stayed there ever since. Clive had even had it hooked up to the electric supply so we could have a little heat for the not so balmy evenings. We often sat there with a gin or whisky, chatting over the day. Sometimes we simply sat in contented silence. The stars seemed to know how to twinkle at their very best when we gazed at them through the doorway, which became a perfect frame. The sun would be warming it in an hour or so, and I'd take my crossword out to my customary seat. It was my dry day habit. People call them Man Caves or She Sheds now, but to us, it will only ever be the Summer House.

The kettle sang and I dropped a teabag into my favourite mug and added the water.

All in all, I was very content with life. I was seventy-two years old and in good health—own hair and mostly my own teeth still intact. My mind was still sharp, and I could exercise regularly, albeit at a gentler pace than in my youth.

My once luxuriant, brown hair may have faded to salt and pepper, but it was still thick. As for the wrinkles around my eyes, they reflected a good and happy life. A happy life, full of laughter with Clive. We'd been married for fifty years, and it felt like five. We'd clicked the first time we met at the Harvest Festival Dance. Our rhythm had matched, and that was that. Married within six months, baby number one just ten months later and baby number two three years after that. Now it seemed strange to think of ourselves not only as parents but also as grandparents and, more recently, even great-grandparents.

Our marriage had healed my family and brought us back together as a whole unit. Clive's support and good sense had helped me accept that my parents, Helen and Francis, were still Mum and Dad despite the biological facts. Our own children had cemented that healing further and we'd reached a place of contentment.

The letterbox clattered, and Benji, our Schnauzer, bounded down the stairs with an energetic bark.

"That's enough, Benji. It's only the post." I removed my teabag, added milk and a spoonful of sugar and went to retrieve the mail from the mat. Benji looked at me expectantly. "There's nothing for you, lad. Go and find Clive." Benji disappeared upstairs again.

I scooped up the post, which was a larger haul than normal and deposited it on the kitchen table. Benji bounded back down the stairs and trotted into the room. He sniffed the air eagerly and tried to jump up to the table. Something obviously smelt good to him and his tiny tail wagged furiously.

"Get down, Benji! You know you're not allowed to do that."

Clive's head appeared around the corner of the door. "Anything interesting in the post, love?"

"I haven't looked yet, but I doubt it. Takeaway menus and flyers for stairlifts seem to be our lot these days."

"Well, you don't need my help to file those in the recycling. I'll take Benji for his walk. Shall I stop off and pick up a couple of cream cakes on the way back?" Clive called Benji over and started to scruff his ears and head with gentle fingers.

"Lovely. Don't forget to take his towel with you. You know he'll only get mud all over the car."

Clive came to my side and planted a kiss on my forehead before whistling. This was Benji's cue. The next few minutes were full of the usual manic excitement he exhibited before any walk. He repeatedly jump-turned as Clive retrieved his lead, ball and poo bags. Trying his best to trip Clive up, Benji started his other favourite game of hurtling from one end of the hall to the other. One of these days, he'd do one of us a serious injury, but we couldn't stop him. There was no point even attempting to do anything until they'd gone. I sipped my tea and waited.

"See you later, love," Clive called, and he and Benji finally left the house.

I allowed the peace and tranquillity to settle. As much as I loved Clive, I did relish these moments of pure silence and the knowledge that I had the house to myself for a good couple of hours. I hummed as I looked through the post. Among the usual junk, there was one weighty envelope with a handwritten name and address. It was thick enough to contain a book. I felt along the sides. Mmm, definitely not a book, and I hadn't ordered anything of late anyway. The envelope was of a quality I hadn't seen since my grandmother's writing box. My humming stopped and my attention was most definitely caught—a real letter. I mean, who even still receives real letters? And more importantly, who still sends them? I turned it over with excitement. Maybe it was a wedding invitation, although I couldn't imagine who from, and it held a mighty gift list if that were the case. I didn't recognise the writing, which was beautiful. Loopy and fluid, it caressed the paper, promising treasures untold inside. The postmark was the only blemish—smudged and messy. It was impossible to make out. I deposited the other less interesting items in the recycling box and retreated to the sunroom with my tea.

Apart from the Summer House, this was my favourite room. It was the house Clive and I had shared since our second child Marianne, had been born. The sunroom ran across the back of the dining room with patio doors onto the garden. We'd had it built a year or so after we first moved in so I could keep an eye on the children as they played.

Now, every house down the street has a conservatory (or garden room as many of them are now known), but I like to think that our little sunroom was the inspiration. We set the ball rolling, you could say. It may be shabby compared to the shiny, sleek UPVC or bi-folding door offerings of the other dwellings, but we love it.

The cushions on the seats have taken on our imprints. You can tell exactly who sits where just by looking at them. Even Benji's bed looks as if it's been there forever. I popped my mug down onto a handmade coaster (a present from my eldest grandchild many years ago) and settled into my chair. I looked at the letter in my hand and was once more struck by the weight of it. It was so intriguing. I slipped my finger under a loose corner and tugged. Inside were fourteen individual letters tied up together with a piece of ribbon. Just by looking at them, I could tell the envelopes were of a similar quality to the one they'd all been posted in. They felt thick and smooth under my fingers. What delights could they hold?

I was thoroughly intrigued now. I couldn't remember the last time I'd received one letter through the post, never mind a bundle of fourteen. In our seventies, we may be, but Clive and our friends have embraced the ease of emails and smart phones. The ribbon was a beautiful shade of green, and that too suggested 'quality' and 'money'. I pulled it loose. The crisp, creamy envelopes fanned out across my knee. They were numbered one to fourteen, and the top one bore the message: 'Read in order – this one first'. The fountain pen had embedded extra emphasis into that short phrase. I needed no more encouragement and tore the envelope open to reveal several sheets of paper.

As I unfolded them, a black and white photograph fluttered onto my lap. I glanced at it—a small child and a lady with a baby on her lap sat at a table laid with a miniature tea set. The lady looked vaguely familiar. I set the photograph on the table and returned to the letter. I was struck again by the beauty of the fluid, dancing letters which formed such tantalising words. But no address or date. What a let-down. I had anticipated every one of the expected writing conventions to be obeyed by someone with such artistic flair. Swallowing my disappointment and another mouthful of tea, I started to read.

Letter Number One

Dear Eve,

I'm not quite sure where or how to begin. What can be said in a handful of letters after all these years? But my time is precious, and I have very little of it left. News of Helen's death was the catalyst, but it's taken until now to react. I had to reach out to you. These words have not been easy to write, and they certainly won't be easy for you to read. Now the moment is actually here, I find myself employing all kinds of delaying tactics. I'm quite unsure where to start. Forgive me.

You probably don't remember me. You were very young when I left. I'm Doris, Aunt Doris, your mother's sister, well actually, your mother in name if not deed. But, of course, you already know that. Helen assured me she would tell you when you came of age and she was never one to break a promise. She was always such a loving sister. Loyalty and family were everything to her, as I'm sure you are only too aware.

The last time I saw you was at Fremell Hall in Oxfordshire. You were very young, coming up for five and your sister less than six months old. I wanted to give you a special parting gift. You see, I was being sent away, my dear. Banished from the family seat, never to darken the doorway again. But I digress.

I'd brought you a little wooden box filled with tiny cups and saucers. An exquisite teapot, milk jug and sugar bowl completed the doll's tea set. Your eyes lit up when you opened it, and you gasped with delight. I've never forgotten the look on your face. It was as if I had given you the world. If only it were so easy.

We sat Teddy and Dolly on cushions at the table and joined them for tea. We enjoyed many cups throughout the morning, and we took it in turns to pour. It's strange the things that have stayed with me over time—Teddy had sugar, Dolly only milk. I vividly remember the beautiful forget-me-not pattern on the china. I'd chosen the pattern deliberately. The enclosed photograph was taken at some point during the tea party. It was the only thing I was allowed to keep. It has been my most treasured possession throughout my life. The material belongings and trappings of wealth I'd enjoyed at the family home were nothing compared to this most precious of items.

All too soon, it was time for me to leave. It was the hardest thing I've ever done. Your parents were kind but firm. There was a limit to how many 'just one more minute' they could endure. I'd tested Helen's love and loyalty to breaking point. I'd tested the family's love and loyalty to breaking point too, and there was no return. It was terribly hard for us all. I'd tried everything in my power to change the outcome, but we had made an agreement and I was left with no choice. The thought of leaving my family home and all that I held dear was devastating, but I'd blown it. Spectacularly! My bridges were well and truly burned and I was left with nothing but cinders.

As the spoilt darling of the household, I was used to getting my own way. It had always been like that. I'd never been encouraged to think about the consequences of my actions or behaviour. I'd certainly never been encouraged to think about the effect these may have on other people. Whatever I'd wanted, I'd taken. This time it was different. With one voice, Mother, Father, Francis and Helen had dug their heels in and refused to listen or give in. During the previous month, I'd veered from anger and frustration to penitence. It was to no avail. My ability to cajole my long-suffering family was suddenly powerless. It was a difficult lesson to learn.

Looking back, I can see I'd always been something of a handful. Times were so different then. Everyone was so rigid and set.

Family name, expectation, reputation and standing were revered, and my parents, particularly my mother, positively worshipped at this altar. Things have changed now. People are far more relaxed and understanding. Back then, society was very unforgiving of anyone who didn't conform. And I was never going to conform, was I?

I'm sorry, Eve. This has exhausted me more than I imagined possible and I need my rest. My mind is starting to fog over, which is a clear sign I need to stop. I will have to tell you about Douglas another day.

Please look after the photograph.

With love,
X

P.S. I have agonised over how to sign off: Aunt Doris? Mother? Mum? None of them seem quite true, but the love most definitely is.

X

CHAPTER 3

I lowered the letter, not knowing quite what to think. Doris. The lady my parents, Helen and Francis, had told me was my real mother. I leant forward and pulled the photograph closer. I could recognise myself in the small child enjoying afternoon tea with Teddy and Dolly. The very same toys had graced our children's and then our grandchildren's beds when they came to stay. My eyes switched to the glamorous lady sitting next to me. She really was exquisite. From her perfectly coifed head to her painted nails, she looked every inch 1950s glamour. Grace Kelly or Elizabeth Taylor could not have looked more lovely. She was smiling brightly and her dimples seemed to fill the picture. My hands raised involuntarily to my own dimples. I'd always presumed I'd inherited them from Grandma, but Doris had clearly passed them on too.

Doris's name had barely been mentioned while I was growing up. The odd occasion when it had come up in conversation was with a whisper and furtive glance. As a result, I knew very little about her despite asking Mum following the big revelation. What she had told me had been general information rather than anything deep and meaningful. Helen and Doris had grown up in a large and comfortable house in Oxfordshire. Actually, house is maybe not the right word. Small, country manor might have been a better description. Not that I knew much about it, nobody had been forthcoming. What was it Doris had called it? I glanced back through her letter and found the name; Fremell Hall.

For some years after her marriage to Francis, Helen had continued to live at the house I must learn to call Fremell Hall with Doris and my grandparents. My father hadn't seen active service during the war. He'd been doing some kind of desk job for the War Office. Like many men from that generation, he'd never really talked about it. He was an upright man who'd taken The Official Secrets Act very seriously, so he was well equipped for dealing with Doris and hers.

Everyone was equally reticent about what had happened to the family property and the wealth that went with it. I have no memories of living in such splendour, although the photograph was obviously taken there. All I do know is by the time Princess Elizabeth had become queen and the country had celebrated her coronation, the family had moved to the Scottish Borders and had been there ever since.

After the birth of our son Rob, I'd been keen to do a bit of family research, but my parents had looked so uncomfortable when I'd mentioned it that I hadn't brought it up again. Tentative questions about Doris had yielded little other than nervous glances and one small titbit of information—Doris was a handful. Of my 'real' father, they refused to speak at all, and my mother had looked so distressed and unwell on the occasion I tried to ask her, I'd allowed the subject to drop. The family were obviously still too ashamed to mention the events surrounding my birth. Times had most definitely changed. Our own great-granddaughter's parents weren't married, but back then, that had been the height of scandal. To a modern generation of gender fluidity, blended and single-sex families, this must seem like a storm in a teacup. Mum and Dad were no longer here to be embarrassed, so maybe now would be a good time to start investigating. Doris's letter seemed to be a sign. I'd give Susan a ring later on.

The glaring question Doris's letter had raised was Douglas. I'd never heard the name mentioned in the family before. Was he, could he be my father? My heart leapt in my chest and a knot of nervous excitement started fluttering around my stomach. Was he the man she'd fallen pregnant to? After all these years, would I finally find out the truth? Don't misunderstand me. Francis had been all the father I'd ever wanted. But Pandora's Box had been opened and it would be nice to know for sure. I hoped the next letter would tell me.

I stretched and winced. One of the disadvantages of old age is how quickly my joints seize up through lack of movement. I braced my hands on the arms of the chair and pushed upward. Allowing myself a few seconds to find my legs, I made my way back into the kitchen. If I had to get up, I might as well use it as a perfect excuse to replenish my tea.

The kettle sat on the Aga once more, and I swilled my mug and added a fresh teabag. Grandmother and Mum had always been so insistent on a real teapot, but Clive and I had lapsed into the modern way years ago. Like everyone of our generation, we were given a beautiful tea service for our wedding. We'd used it frequently at first, but now it spent its days in the display cupboard only coming out for high days and holidays. Our main objection isn't to the teapot itself; it's the size of the cups. They are so tiny compared to the generous hand-warming mugs we use now. Maybe I should dig the old teapot out for later, I mused as I poured the water onto the waiting bag.

While the tea brewed, I was suddenly struck by the most important question of all. How on earth had it not struck me sooner? Doris was dead. My parents had told me that the same day they'd revealed my true parentage. As the teabag and water became one, I was transported back to that morning at my parents' house.

Helen had crossed the room to join me by the window. She'd reached out her arms tentatively and, feeling no resistance, pulled me close to her. For some time, we had stayed there, allowing our tears to soak each other's shoulders.

When Helen had finally pulled away, she'd told me that my real mother was her sister Doris. Her beautiful younger sister, who had horrified the family by falling pregnant while unmarried. It was obviously still painful for Helen to talk about as she had shuddered following this disclosure. She'd thrown a worried glance at my father, who had nodded encouragement. As she and

Francis were already married, it had made sense for them to adopt me.

Somehow, and I never got to the bottom of this, the village never suspected. As far as they were concerned, little Eve was the delightful offspring of Helen and Francis. Doris had moved away from the family just before I turned five and had tragically died in a car accident in Australia not long after arriving there. Her car had been involved in a collision with a kangaroo, and the kangaroo had won. Helen had been quite matter of fact about it. In her will, Doris had stipulated that I be told the truth when I came of age. Helen and Francis had followed her wishes despite knowing it could change our relationship irrevocably. Luckily, with time and healing, it hadn't.

The kitchen came back into focus and so did my thoughts. If Doris was dead, how on earth could she be sending me post? I walked quickly back to the sunroom, stiff joints well and truly forgotten and snatched up the letter again. No address or date, but the references to years passing, old age and precious time led me to believe that the writer was still very much alive, albeit near the end of life. Either way, this was not the letter of a young woman who had just moved to Australia. I checked the envelope again, and the postmark still mocked me with its indecipherable smudge. There was no accompanying note of explanation inside. What the hell was going on? How on earth could Doris, a woman who had died sixty-odd years ago, be writing to me? I didn't like this one little bit. What had started as a bit of nostalgia and intrigue was turning decidedly sinister. I wished Clive would come back.

I dropped the letter onto the table and returned to the kitchen. I went through the motions of removing the teabag, adding milk and sugar and stirring. My hands were shaky and my mind was in overdrive. How could one small letter throw up so many questions? And what on earth would be revealed next?

As much as the prospect filled me with dread, there was only one way to find out.

Letter Number Two

Dearest Eve,

I'm sure the first letter coming out of the blue like that has left you with many questions. I can't imagine my years of exile have been full of family chatter about me. I'm not bitter, my dear. I brought it upon myself.

From the wisdom of old age, I can see that even as a child, I was a spoilt handful. A little madam, some may say. Before the wars, our parents lived in a beautiful large house with staff to look after our every need. Mother and Father were not obliged to get involved in the drudgery of child rearing. All they had to do was enjoy their pretty daughters. As one of the notable families in the area, our lives consisted of social events and pleasure. Our days were a series of picnics on the terrace or lawn, exploring the gardens or being driven out with Mother to visit one of her friends. It was all sickeningly idyllic. Oh, there had been dark times too, believe me. During World War One, our home had been requisitioned as a military hospital. Mother spoke of that time with compressed lips. Not surprisingly, keeping the heirlooms in one piece had been far less of a priority than piecing the poor men back together. Apparently, the Hall had been quite a wreck when peace was declared. But, the Monmouths had bounced back. By the time Helen and I were approaching five and seven, Fremell Hall was restored to its former glory. It was in this environment that we grew up.

Helen had very much been the apple of our parents' eye, but there's no denying that I eclipsed her to become the one they truly doted on. Father was utterly besotted and determined to let his little girl have everything she desired. Even Mother roused herself from self-absorption to take delight in me—she liked to show me off. Time and distance have forced many a realisation upon me, one of which being my parents' behaviour. I can see that this was, in part, responsible for the tale I'm setting down in these letters.

My family were rich, comfortable and content. The village respected our parents and admired their offspring. Helen and I were known as the Marvellous Monmouths. Our long, brunette curls which hinted at glimpses of burnished copper and red, were very much admired. Mother always ensured that our clothes were impeccable and our posture exemplary. We were her greatest showpieces. Although Helen was a very pretty girl, I had beauty with a capital B. I'd inherited my mother's dimples, and they were an extremely useful weapon. My unusual hazel eyes framed by impossibly long lashes only added to my charms.

The real success when it came to securing devotion was that hard to describe phenomena known as charisma. Whatever it is, I had it in bucket loads and still do. From an early age, Mother capitalised on this powerful attribute; she had it to a lesser degree herself, and she wasn't averse to using it to get her own way. I observed her successes and cultivated them for myself, but I'll return to that later.

World War II changed everything again. Whereas the first war had turned our house into a military hospital, the second had decimated our workforce. During the war years, it was impossible to find enough staff; the young and able men were off to fight, and the women were drafted into other war effort activities. Mother had to grow accustomed to fending for herself, something she was more than capable of but would rather not have to! Helen and I learnt life skills which, though dull and boring, were extremely useful. We came to rely even more heavily upon our housekeeper Mary.

Mary had grown up at Fremell Hall. Her mother Joan, or Mrs Hardcastle as we always called her, had been our housekeeper first. Mary's father Bill, who for some reason we never called Mr Hardcastle, was our head gardener. Having survived a mustard gas attack and the horrors of the not so Great War, Bill's health never really recovered. Father ensured that his role became one of delegation instead of physical labour, and Mother employed Mary as a housemaid to safeguard her future. For more years than anyone thought possible, Bill creaked on. Mary proved an exemplary member of staff and was learning how to be as accomplished a housekeeper as her mother. She also became a confidante to Helen and I, and it seemed perfectly natural to tell her our childish worries.

Bill's death was a huge blow to Mrs Hardcastle. She was utterly distraught and seemed to disintegrate before our eyes. The calm, unflappable woman who had stoically pulled up her sleeves to assist with the gore and horror of the military hospital was gone. It soon became apparent that she would be unable to carry on running Fremell Hall. When she told Mother that her other daughter had invited her to live with her and her husband, we all dreaded her departure. We dreaded Mary's departure as well. Good, reliable staff were increasingly difficult to find. Although Mary was young to be offered the role of housekeeper, Mother had no misgivings. We all knew she'd had excellent training. She was loyal, efficient and had inherited Mrs Hardcastle's mouth-watering culinary skills. As for Mary, she was only too happy to remain in the only home she'd known with a secure future.

Like Mrs Hardcastle before Bill's death, she was calm and competent, and she became even more integral to our lives. She was hardworking and utterly devoted to the Monmouth family. My parents trusted her implicitly and so did Helen and I. Mary was the one we continued to turn to with our secrets. Mother wasn't the type to encourage anyone to share their woes, and she certainly didn't encourage her daughters to indulge in gossip or needless chit-chat. With Mary, it was different. Helping stir her famous soup had a wonderful way of loosening our tongues. No problem we took to her was too big to solve. She was part of the fabric of the Hall just as surely as we were.

During the Second World War, Mary oversaw the growing of vegetables in our walled garden, and it was she who fed the chickens and made the rations stretch further than we thought possible. Although the war was a terrible time, in other ways, it was wonderful. The sense of community and pulling together was strong and everyone did their bit. Mother warmed to her role as Lady Benevolent and distributed food parcels made up of vegetables we'd grown. Extra eggs from our chickens were made available to those in need. On the odd occasion, Mother even collected the eggs herself. She was also on the committee, which helped organise events at the village hall. And it was during this time I met Douglas.

From the first moment I saw him, I knew I wanted him. The fact he was stepping out with Margaret Holland was immaterial. The night I met him, the family were attending the local Serviceman's Dance. The war had been on for five years, and there was an air base not far away. Our village took the entertainment of these brave and handsome young men very seriously. As the notable family in the area and with Mother on the organisation committee, we always attended to show support for 'Our Boys'.

That night my hair gleamed in its stylish victory rolls and my outfit belied the ration books and coupons that most women were restricted by. The Monmouths had money, a respectable name, and a stack of silk and fine fabrics jealously guarded from previous generations. Helen and I never had to adopt the wartime drab. It had clearly worked for Helen, who was accompanied by her new husband, Francis. She looked radiant. I had decided that night it was my turn to find love.

Douglas caught my eye as soon as we walked in. Tall, enigmatic and handsome, he oozed confidence, and I was instantly smitten. Even better, he was too. We danced and talked and that was that. Our rhythm just seemed to match. I hope you have found this kind of happiness, Eve. Obviously, Margaret wasn't pleased when Douglas told her it was over between them. As the eldest daughter of the next notable family to ours, we'd always been friendly rivals. Now, she could barely look at me if our paths crossed in the village. I was totally unrepentant. Douglas loved me and that was all that mattered.

It was a whirlwind romance, and his proposal came just two weeks after we met. I didn't hesitate. I really do think relationships were entered into and flourished in a far better way back then. Now, couples wait for years deciding if they will be compatible or whether they should go to the next level, whatever that is. Live for the moment was the wartime motto. It certainly worked for our generation. I was so happy and so in love. He made me feel incredibly alive. Wedding plans and baby plans filled my days. The desire for a family with Douglas became my reason for living. It also gave me something to do during the agony of waiting. Every time his squadron flew out, we knew they might not all return. Yet I couldn't believe that would actually happen. Not to me.

Douglas had the date for his final mission and we were to be married straight after. Mother and Helen were busy with dress patterns while I finalised plans with the vicar. We were going to hold a special Wedding Dance for the whole village. My heart was full. The blow, when it came, was crushing.

'Regret to inform. Captain Douglas Bennett dead. Shot down. France.'

Douglas was dead. My world broke and my heart

shattered. Our lovely golden future turned black before my eyes. The longed-for wedding and family had been snatched away. I was beyond grief. Never in my life had my will been thwarted. Never had I not got my own way. Who had dared to interfere and spoil my well thought out plans? Somehow my parents carried me up to my room, where I gave way to grief.

Why him? He was mine. He was not to be taken by anyone else. The pain in my chest was incredible. It burned and engulfed me as poor Douglas must have been inside his tiny tin cockpit. Shot down in flames of disbelief, I let the tears consume me.

"Darling, how about a nice cup of tea?" Helen's voice was distorted through the bedroom door. As she slowly opened it, I turned away from her and she left the teacup on the bedside table.

Over the next few days, the household tiptoed around me. Helen or Mary held me as I wept, sometimes tears of anger, sometimes of grief. Even Mother, who found emotional displays uncomfortable, sat with me and brushed the tears from my cheeks. Father patted my hand but was unable to offer any words of hope or help. I didn't want them anyway. Francis, so utterly out of his comfort zone, took care of practicalities like retrieving Douglas's belongings from the airbase. The day that pitiful bundle arrived, I wept afresh. How could such a vital, joyful life be represented by so few things?

Days turned into weeks and eventually months, and I still refused to leave my room. I spent hours sitting by the window looking at the sky as if this would somehow bring me closer to him. The gulf had never been wider. Every day, Mary knocked tentatively on my door, trying to tempt my lost appetite with the best that rations could provide. I returned the meals mostly uneaten, which was such a terrible waste in a time of privation.

Just when the family started to fear for my reason, I decided to re-join life again. I would mope around no more. Life was still to be lived. Douglas had been a fairytale, but I lived in a world that was less happy ever after and more count your blessings. I was young, I was beautiful, and the much longed-for family could still be achieved. The plan would still happen; it would just need executing differently. I thought about little else over the next few months. Doris Monmouth was not to be deterred by war, grief or anybody.

Forgive me for stopping again, my dear. As you can see, my writing is deteriorating, and my hand simply can't keep up with my thoughts. I need to gather my strength in more ways than one. These events may have happened over seventy-five years ago, but the pain has never truly gone. Plus, this will allow you a chance to digest what you have read.

Fill your teapot or lamentable mug as people use these days and turn to the next letter when you are ready.

Much love,
X

CHAPTER 5

My tears had fallen regularly as I read. It was so tragic and so poignant. I wiped my face and lowered the letter to my lap. Sobs caught in my ribs and I gulped them down.

Doris's pain and anguish had touched me profoundly. Her description of her love for Douglas felt like mine for Clive. Although Doris's name had been so seldom mentioned and the few times it had, had been surrounded by unease and tension, I felt nothing but sympathy for her. To lose the love of your life before you'd even had a chance to marry and have children must be doubly heart-breaking. I could understand her anguish. My heart contracted with fear when I thought about life without my lovely Clive. I was so lucky that our rhythm had matched and remained. We were so much more fortunate than Doris and Douglas had been.

I wish my mother had told me more about this woman who was part of my DNA. Why had they struck her from the family memory? Why had they told me she was dead when it was obvious from these letters that she was very much alive? So many unanswered questions. My parents were reasonable, calm and caring people, so I was struggling to understand it all. I was struggling to suppress my anger too. It seemed they had deliberately deceived me. And what about Douglas? Was this much-loved man my father? Maybe I had unknown cousins who I could reach out to. I couldn't understand why my parents hadn't told me about him either. More anger flickered within me.

I came back to earth with a bump. What a fool you are, Eve, I chided myself. The dates made it impossible for Douglas to be my father. That mystery was still to be solved.

I was getting stiff again, and I wished I could cancel my membership to the 'Getting Older Club'. With a creaky stretch, I made my way to the bathroom before returning to the kitchen.

Reading Doris's letter highlighted the fact that teapots, cups and saucers used to be the norm. Pretty crockery that felt delicate on the lips was a must in every household in my youth. I couldn't remember the last time we'd used ours but now seemed a good opportunity. Our beautiful wedding gift, it would be nice to get it out for once. I drew the line at the small cup and saucer, but I would use the china teapot to fill my 'lamentable' mug.

The display cabinet in the dining room showed off the set to perfection. The teapot takes pride of place in the centre, and the cups, saucers, jugs and sugar bowl make a symmetrical pattern around it. I must have dusted this cabinet hundreds of times and become immune to the beauty of the tea service. Looking at it with fresh eyes, I could see it really was very pretty with delicate blue flowers that clung to the china like petals to a stalk. It would all need a bit of rinse, though. I retrieved the china I'd need and carried it carefully to the kitchen sink. I filled the washing up bowl with soapy water and plunged the teapot in first. I swooshed it around the soap suds, rinsed it and turned it over to let the water out. It was then I noticed the words 'Forget-me-not' on the bottom. Well, that was fitting. I'm sure Doris would approve.

If I was going to use the teapot, I decided I may as well go the whole hog and make the tea properly. I warmed the pot and even found some loose-leaf tea at the back of the cupboard. I sniffed it cautiously. The original box bearing the best before date was long gone, but it still smelt like tea, so I couldn't see the harm in using it. I ladled in a spoon and a half for good measure and poured on the water. While it brewed, I loaded a tray with the pot, tea strainer, sugar bowl and matching milk jug. Admittedly, my mug looked a little incongruous, but I wasn't ready to forego it just yet. As a concession, I'd chosen a china mug instead of my usual boldly patterned, chunky one. I would normally have slipped a couple of biscuits onto a plate, but I'd save myself for the cream cakes when Clive got back. I checked the clock; he shouldn't be too much longer.

The Summer House would be just about perfect now. The sun had moved around, and the cedar would be giving off its heady scent as the rays warmed it. Giving the pot a final stir, I picked up the tray and carried it carefully through the sunroom, across the garden and into the Summer House. The late spring sunshine was warm, but the air was still chilly and I was glad to step inside our little suntrap. With the tray in place on the table, I made my way back across the grass to retrieve Doris's letters. I gathered them all up in case I needed to refer back to any of them as her story developed.

The tea made a satisfying sound as it danced its way into my mug. It certainly seemed more special than a soggy teabag. Maybe this was the way forward. I must remember to buy some more loose-leaf next time I went shopping. Ensconced in my chair, I picked up the third letter. I hoped this would contain a happier tale for Doris. Losing Douglas had been such a blow to her and I really hoped she'd found happiness with someone else. More importantly, though, I was hoping to find out about my father.

I tugged open the envelope and unfolded the paper.

"Right then, Doris, let's see what you've got for us this time!"

Letter Number Three

Dearest Eve,

I have passed over that time of utter grief and despair. These days, I'd have been given scream therapy or painting pots before smashing them to get rid of my anger and pain. Back then, you just got on with it. The stiff upper lip was everything. After all, I wasn't the only girl to lose a sweetheart in the conflict. War is a terrible thing.

After a few months of staring into the abyss, I made up my mind that grief would get me nowhere. I had to think of the future. My plans for a family could still go ahead. It was time to move on. Douglas slipped further and further away until I convinced myself his memory didn't seem to be there anymore. I could still get everything I wanted, and I would.

It was a sunny spring day in 1946, and the Monmouths were due at the village hall. The Serviceman's Dance had become the Ex-Serviceman's Dance and was still held two or three times a year. Helen knocked on my bedroom door to ask if I would like to come. After months of flat refusals, she was surprised and relieved to find me putting the finishing touches to my hair.

Lovely Helen, married to Francis, who looked at her as if she was the first prize in a race he'd never imagined winning. He was a good, kind man and he was devoted to Helen, and she was equally devoted to him. I've just realised how silly I sound. After all, you know this far better than I. They too had dreams of babies. As yet, nothing had happened, but their time would come, just as mine would.

My parents were delighted to see I would be accompanying them. Father because his darling girl was attempting to smile again. Mother because she would no longer have to make small talk about

34

'poor Doris' and why I'd stayed at home. The fact that the whole family would be on display to the village pleased her no end. My mother loved playing Lady of the Manor, and she regarded mine and Helen's beauty as her own personal achievement. There's no denying she was a very attractive woman.

It was pleasant to stroll through the village within the protective circle of my family. Caps were raised to us and smiles thrown our way by all we passed. I was surprised at how much I was enjoying myself. Life was definitely still for the living. The evening would be a success, I could tell.

The village hall was decked with bunting and victory posters, and it was already busy when we arrived. The crowds made way for us as my father ushered us through. Like many places since the war, there had been changes to the local population. More than ever, people moved where the jobs were. The rural villages like ours were welcoming farm workers and craftsmen aplenty. There were some new faces in the room tonight.

I spotted him straight away. He was standing on the other side of the dance floor, neatly dressed and handsome in a quirky kind of way. His hair was dark and wavy like mine. Tall, lean but strong and graceful, he was ticking all the boxes so far. Even better, he was one of the new faces.

I just needed to speak to him. But that had never proved a barrier before. My face, with its flirtatious dimples, was generally enough to make most men try to engage me in conversation. Even those who weren't at liberty to do so couldn't help themselves. As expected, he soon glanced over and made his way around to my side. I was relieved to hear his voice was well-modulated, and he was clearly intelligent. His teeth were truly beautiful.

What had seemed like a difficult task was now very much achievable. He proved himself a competent dancer, and he made me genuinely laugh on more than one occasion. He had been visiting one of the farms to conduct a survey on the building. He was scheduled to come back in a couple of weeks. At least, I think that's what he said. To be frank, I wasn't overly interested in what he did, although my ears did prick up about his plans to return. Overall, he was good company. Our rhythm didn't match exactly, but it was close enough.

As always, at these events, our parents left early. Father believed that the locals wouldn't truly let their hair down while he and Mother were still there. This was just an excuse. The truth was, dancing wasn't his thing. As for Mother, her love of it was overruled by her snobbery. To be seen dancing with the local yokels was simply not for her. This was one trait I was glad I hadn't inherited. I loved dancing and was quite content to be twirled around by my new companion.

Convincing him that I needed someone to walk me home at the end of the evening was hardly a challenge either. Men are so easily led, even the smart ones. I played my part to perfection. Shy, flattering and apparently interested in what he had to say, he was an easy fish to reel in.

Of course, he wanted to see me again. He was keen to call on me at the house, but that wasn't what I wanted just yet. I convinced him that meeting by the river when he was next in the village would be much more romantic. There was a beautiful weeping willow on the bend of the river. Next to it was a bench set at just the right angle to admire the view. A mixture of cultivated and wildflowers mingled and turned that whole stretch into an oasis of beauty and wildlife. That would be the setting for our rendezvous. I allowed him to kiss my cheek before pressing a quick kiss of my own onto his lips. I pulled away, lowered my eyes and allowed my dimples to peep.

He was a perfectly nice man, Eve. Personable, good company and intelligent. I have asked myself why I treated him so very badly and I have searched deep within myself for answers over the years. Some are more satisfactory than others. This probably seems like the admission of a cold-hearted woman, which I'm not. I loved Douglas passionately. As much as I tried to convince myself I was moving on and getting over him, my love for him was all-consuming. I suppose nobody could ever have lived up to this. Robert certainly couldn't, but he did his poor best.

I apologise for breaking off once more. Recounting just this small part of my life story is proving exhausting. Goodness knows how people can bear to write autobiographies. I can think of nothing more tedious than being faced with a lifetime of terrible choices and mistakes to justify and uphold.

I will tell you more about Robert in the next letter, I promise.

Lots of love,
X

CHAPTER 7

With a sigh, I lowered Doris's letter to my lap. How could these few pages contain copious amounts of information and so many unanswered questions in equal measure? My head was starting to spin with it all.

It looked as if Doris had moved on from Douglas's death. I was glad she had emerged from seclusion and was ready to join reality once more. But reading on, I realised it wouldn't be that simple. The more I read, the less I felt I understood her. She was multi-layered, with each letter peeling away to reveal something new and unexpected below. On the surface, I should have felt relief that she'd met an apparently nice man. So why did my stomach churn with anxiety? What on earth was still to come?

She mentioned the name Robert which is the name Clive and I had chosen for our son. A good Scottish name that can be shortened in many ways. Our son had been Robbie to us until he settled on Rob in his teenage years.

I cast my mind back to the day when our Robbie was born. Giving birth was a very different experience back then. There was no such thing as a birth plan, labour playlist or birthing partners, and Clive wasn't even allowed in the room. Instead, he paced the corridor outside, eagerly awaiting news. When the nurse told him he had a son and he was allowed in the room to be at my side, we cried tears of joy. Our first born. Our son. Our Robbie. We'd discussed a whole myriad of names in the preceding months. We definitely wanted something Scottish, and it had to be something that sounded good with our surname Gilchrist. We'd both agreed on Robert. And, of course, in the days before smartphones, it was Clive who went to phone the family.

The memory of my parents' reaction seemed to catapult itself into the Summer House. I remember Clive telling me about it. They'd been overjoyed. Bubbling with excitement, they'd eagerly asked about the sex, time, weight, and of course, name. Having gushed over the news that we had a boy born at 10.23 in the morning, weighing 7lb 3 oz, their reaction to his name had seemed odd. Clive told me the line had gone so quiet he thought they'd been cut off. He'd repeated Robert's name and after a pause, my mother had just said, 'That's nice'. Given that hippy names for babies were starting to become popular, I thought they'd have welcomed our conventional and traditional choice. Clive and I had definitely been a bit hurt at the time, but we put it down to over sensitivity caused by fatigue.

Nearly fifty years later, it was starting to make sense. If this man Robert was my father, the name must have been a constant reminder of Doris's indiscretion and the shame she'd brought upon the family. On the other hand, if this man really was my father, I was glad we'd given his name to our son. What could be more fitting than Robert Francis Alexander being named after all three of his grandfathers?

I glanced back through the letter and was drawn to the line 'I have asked myself why I treated him so very badly' and contemplated what that could mean. Doris may be proving hard to understand, but the one thing that had definitely struck me was her force of character. Doris was clearly a woman who knew what she wanted and generally got it.

As much as I longed to find out, part of me dreaded it. I wasn't sure if I was ready for any more revelations just yet. I needed a break and not just for tea. There was enough left in the pot to last. I refilled my mug and took it for a walk around the garden.

Normally on these perambulations, I'd stop at various plants and flowers to examine their progress and growth. Sometimes, I'd stoop to remove a misplaced weed but not this time. This time I was content to feel the springy grass under my shoes and welcome the sun on my skin. I tried to empty my mind, but it was harder than I imagined. No amount of yoga classes I'd dabbled with over the years had prepared me for a pack of letters from my past.

So many thoughts chased each other; Doris, Robert,

my parents, my grandmother. The grandmother I knew seemed very different from the woman Doris was portraying in her letters. I got the distinct impression there was a lot of tension in their relationship.

Then there was Robert himself. My parents had told me categorically they didn't know who my father was—given their reaction when we named our son, that now seemed highly unlikely. Suddenly, everything I thought I knew was up for debate. Was anything in my life actually true?

I turned to face the back of our house. Solid, homely, dependable. Our house. Mine and Clive's. That was true. Clive and I and our love for each other, that was also true. Our children Rob and Marianne, also true. Our wonderful grandchildren and great-grandchild were all true and good and precious. It was just what came before that wasn't.

Tension in my stomach knotted and formed a tight ball. Something that felt like frustration tinged with anger flickered within me. I had to suppress it quickly. I couldn't allow it to take over, not after all these years. I placed my mug on the grass and stretched my hands high above my head. I concentrated on my breathing for a minute. In with calm, out with anger. My mantra worked and the flicker died. I circled my shoulders and felt them crunch. My eyes felt heavy, and I rubbed them though nothing was clearer when I dropped my hands back to my sides. I picked up my mug and looked at the Summer House. It was time to return to the muddy waters of my past. I crossed the threshold.

The pile of letters seemed to taunt me like a playground bully. I knew I had to get past, but it was going to take courage. I took a breath and drew the next envelope toward me. My chair welcomed me, and my fingers tore across the flap and around the back of the paper. A jagged tear appeared across Doris's firm print 'Letter Number Four'. It was time to set the contents free.

Letter Number Four

Darling Eve,

I'm sure you long to hear about Robert and have many questions about him. I imagine your first question is regarding your parentage, and you are quite right with your assumption; Robert was your father.

Our meeting on the bench next to the weeping willow was everything I hoped it would be. Robert was punctual and armed with flowers he'd picked along the way. Life was simpler then without bouquets of specially grown unique buds and greenery. He'd just gathered the flowers he'd found along the paths and riverside. He was smartly turned out and his shoes were beautifully polished. Your grandfather always said you could tell a lot about a man by how he kept his shoes. Robert's were shiny and it even looked as if the shoe's laces had been ironed, no doubt a throwback to days in the army. He greeted me with a brief peck on the cheek. His eyes crinkled as he smiled. He was really rather attractive.

We sat and watched the wind dancing through the low hanging leaves. The tips dipped into the river like ballet dancers entering a swimming pool. He asked about my family and my life. I did tell him about Douglas, but it was an edited version. Stupidly I thought Douglas had been removed from my thoughts but telling Robert about him brought him back with a jolt. Talking about my darling to another man seemed disloyal, if not downright unfaithful. I knew I would have to get over these emotions to fulfil my wish.

As soon as I could, I turned the conversation back around. Robert told me a little about his family. Good, solid, dependable—his words, not mine. Living comfortably in Liverpool, they'd suffered terrible losses during the war. The family home, 'Nice but not as grand as yours Doris', had been destroyed in a direct hit courtesy of the Luftwaffe. Sadly or perhaps mercifully, his mother and younger sister had died instantly. His father had been patrolling the streets with the Volunteer Corps that night and came home to a ruined life. Robert, caught up in fighting in France, had received the distressing news via telegram. How I remember the impact of stark words on a crisp bit of paper heralding misery, hurt and pain. My heart flipped and seemed to land in my stomach. My own loss seemed almost sharper in that moment than on the day it had actually happened. But at least I still had my family. Robert had lost his. His father had suffered a stroke three months later and never really recovered. He died just before the war ended.

With no family home to return to and a city of rubble and bomb pits as a welcome, Robert had moved to the Welsh Borders and returned to work as an architect. How he could bear to build homes and houses knowing his had been turned to rubble was beyond me. Yes, my little world had been turned upside down when Douglas died, but the fabric of my life remained. My safe haven, Fremell Hall, was still there and had cocooned me during those initial weeks and months after his death. No bombs had touched our village at all. The village green was still serene, the ducks still gathered in hopes of bread at 3.30 each afternoon, and the church clock still struck the hour and half hour as it had always done. The make-up of the village looked exactly the same now as it had before the war. The only change was the addition of a second memorial to mark our dead and the missing faces in church on Sundays.

The horrors of the air raids were beamed into our houses via the wireless radio. We'd crowd around it each night desperate for news. We sympathised during those dreadful months of the Blitz but couldn't truly imagine it. Robert's simple, matter of fact words left a big impression upon me. I placed my gloved hand on his arm by way of support. His hand covered mine and he gave me a wistful smile. I was in danger of falling for him. Douglas was still there. His face *and features would never be forgotten, but Robert was shifting my focus.*

Our courtship had begun.

It was different this time. There was no wartime frenzy to hurry us along and, despite taking to Robert, I refused to give my heart entirely. Whether the bit I kept back was for me or Douglas, I'm still not entirely sure. My family, of course, were delighted and relieved in equal measure. Thoughts of me growing into a faded spinster had worried Mother. Whatever would people think? My mother's obsession with caring what others thought often brought us into conflict, so it was a relief to have this particular battle declared a truce. The other battle we faced was Robert's background.

Although of a good social standing in Liverpool, he was definitely a rung or two below the Monmouths as far as Mother was concerned. Her utter relief when he spoke without the famous Liverpool accent could be felt by everyone, including Robert, who simply switched on his charming smile to disarm her. I'm sure he must have thought her a terrible snob. In normal circumstances, she would have undoubtedly questioned my choice, but the war had taken too many young and eligible men. Plus, society was starting to shift with the new sands the war had brought, and Mother was carried along like everyone else.

His proposal when it came was simple and not unexpected. You could even say I'd been waiting for it. Everything was done by the book. My father's permission was sought and given in the study as expected. I wonder, did your husband ask Francis for your hand? I remember my father calling me into the room then stepping forward to formally present my hand to Robert like I was some kind of possession. It all sounds so archaic now, but it was just the way of the world back then.

And so, part one of my plan was complete. Or so I thought. While I had been arranging my future exactly as I wished, a tragedy was about to occur in Helen's world—something that would rock us and set my mind in overdrive. It was a tragedy that would have huge implications for us all.

I must break off again, Eve. The doctors have told me I mustn't exert myself. Who would have thought putting pen to paper could be so exhausting. Until the last few years, I was still walking five miles every day. I've been active, fit and healthy my whole life, and to find myself exhausted by writing a mere letter is frustrating beyond belief. The wretched Old Age Club has welcomed me in with open arms. They should have saved themselves the bother. It's not a club I want anything to do with, but as I've learnt over the years, some things I can't have all my own way.

The next letter will, I'm sure, make difficult reading but it has to be written.

Love always
X

CHAPTER 9

When I'd picked up my past from the post on the mat this morning, little had I realised the questions, emotions and confusion it would reveal. In a short space of time, I'd discovered my birth mother was still very much alive and my birth father was a decent man called Robert who had apparently loved her but had disappeared from the scene. There were so many things that needed answering. Why had Doris been exiled? What had happened to Robert, and why had I been adopted by Helen and Francis? And of course, why my parents and indeed Grandmother had lied to me about Doris still being very much alive. I felt cheated. Not that I would have wanted a relationship with her necessarily, but it would have been nice to have been given the option. Now I just had growing resentment about secrets that had been kept from me.

A welcome diversion bounded into the Summer House. Benji was back from his walk and came to greet me with his usual enthusiasm. With a lolling tongue, he ran around my chair and pushed himself into my legs for a fuss. The letter on my lap was of great interest to him, and he sniffed it eagerly and tried to jump up.

"No, Benji, that's enough. Lie down!" Benji took no notice and continued to sniff. "Lie down, Benji." I used my no-nonsense voice, and he responded with that look all dog owners are familiar with—the look of deep hurt and reproach. Why do they always make you feel so damned guilty?

Benji settled by my feet with his head facing the door. He was sulking. The sulks ended when Clive emerged from the sunroom and made his way across the grass with a couple of plates and a paper bag. Benji raised his head and yawned.

"Ready for your cream cake, love?" Clive appeared directly in the doorway and momentarily blocked the light. I'd never been so relieved to see him. "Are you all right, Eve? You don't look quite yourself."

"Myself! I don't even know who myself is anymore, Clive!" I bit my lip and could feel my lip quivering. Clive deposited the cakes on the table, sat down and reached for my hands.

"What's happened? Do you feel ill?"

"It's these dreadful letters from Aunt Doris, well, my mother. They are full of stuff, family stuff and revelations, shocking revelations. The life I thought I knew was a lie." I was barely coherent.

"Aunt Doris? What letters? Eve, you aren't making any sense."

"I know I'm not, but I don't know how to make sense of it. Doris is still alive. The woman who gave birth to me and gave me to Helen and Francis did not die in Australia decades ago. I don't even know if she's actually in Australia. For all I know, she could have been living up the road all these years." Tears fell down my face, filled with anger, grief and confusion.

I pulled my hands away from Clive and clenched my fingers in an attempt to control myself. Clive looked stunned, as well he might. He opened his mouth then obviously thought better of it. I was so glad he wasn't bombarding me with questions I didn't know the answers to. Kind, logical and measured Clive, who never rushed into emotional situations with knee-jerk reactions. No wonder he'd made such a good GP. No wonder he'd been so good for me. I looked at the man who'd been by my side for more than fifty years and felt grounded. This was the world I knew. This was my life. A shaky breath drew some much-needed oxygen into my lungs. He had to know, but the thought of telling him all the information I'd just absorbed was beyond me at the moment.

"I'll tell you properly, Clive, I promise, but I need a minute."

"Would a cup of tea help?" I nodded. "Right, two cups of tea and two cream cakes coming right up. Crikey Eve, why have you got the old teapot out here? Were you expecting the queen?"

"It's a long story. I'll tell you later."

While Clive busied himself loading the tray, I thought back over the letters I'd read. Their contents had rocked my world and left me dazed. What on earth had happened to Robert? Where was Doris now, and what was the tragedy Helen had undergone? I hoped the remaining letters would give me some answers. The little of Doris I knew was warning me to prepare myself for yet more shocks. I had to know, but I dreaded it at the same time.

I bent over to stroke Benji's head. I pulled his ears gently through my fingers and felt myself calming down. Sitting back up, I gathered the letters I'd already opened and pushed them to Clive's side of the table. I couldn't face going over the contents with him. He could read them, just as I had. I looked towards the house and saw him heading my way with the tea. The fancy pot had been left inside, and our usual mugs were held tightly in his hands. Arthritis was starting to affect his grip and he took his time.

"I hope you don't mind, I left the pot inside. I thought this would be quicker." He placed the mugs on the table and sat down. I busied myself unwrapping the cakes and depositing them on the plates. A blob of cream caught on my thumb and I licked it clean. "Do you want to tell me about it? I'm guessing the post was more exciting than stairlift flyers after all."

"Just a bit!" I replied with wry humour. I took a breath. "Ok, here's the short version. My birth mother, Doris, you remember, she was Mum's sister, isn't dead.

She's been alive and well for all these years, and she's written me a bundle of letters with revelations from her past and mine too. I've found out who my father was but not what happened to him. There's definitely something not right about that, but I have no idea what. I'm only halfway through the letters and part of me is dreading opening the next one."

"Alive?! But I thought she died when you were a child?" Not surprisingly, Clive looked incredulous.

"You and me both. Turns out, that's just one of the many untruths in this life I thought was mine."

"And your father, not Francis, your birth father? You said you know who he is too?"

"Yes, a man called Robert. Look, Clive, I can't go through all this again. Why don't you take the letters and read them yourself? I have to carry on with the others."

Clive took a generous bite of his cake. He always did this when he wanted to think before answering. If no beverage or foodstuff was around to create a delay, he simply left the other person hanging in limbo. It could be absolutely infuriating. He licked his lips.

"Ok, Eve, I'll just finish this and then I think it's best if I take the letters inside. You know I can't concentrate when you are reading in the same room."

This was one of our many standing jokes. Unlike Clive, who immersed himself fully in books, newspapers and screens, I found it impossible to read without gasping at revelations and vocalising my feelings. I made it impossible for anyone else in the room to focus on what they were doing. I gave him a loving smile.

"These are the ones I've read so far." I handed the ragged envelopes to him. "I've put them back in order for you. But Doris has left strict instructions in case you get muddled."

"Doris has? Er ok, I'll take those now. Don't forget your cake. You've not touched it yet."

Clive stretched out a hand and I put mine gratefully inside his. My safe haven. We squeezed and let go. He gathered up the letters and stacked his mug on top of his plate.

"I'll be in the sunroom if you need me."

"Thank you, darling. I love you."

"I love you too, now don't forget to eat."

I couldn't face food even though my rumbling stomach suggested otherwise. I took a single bite to appease it and pulled the next letter toward me. I felt like Alice at the top of the rabbit hole. Here goes, deep breath and dive in.

Letter Number Five

Dearest Eve,

Before I tell you about Helen's tragedy, I feel I should explain a little more about your grandmother and the kind of relationship we had with her. By the time I left, she was a very different woman from the one we had grown up with.

In many ways she was an admirable woman. Incredibly attractive, strong, loyal and utterly devoted to upholding the family name. She had married slightly above herself, as society delighted in saying back then, making her into an incurable snob. This was one of the reasons she had looked so scant at Robert. 'Be as I say, not as I am!' was her motto for life. Petrified of doing or saying something which would highlight her real social standing to the general public, she adhered by the letter to the conventions of the day.

Although she did not show it, she loved our father and was a dutiful wife, and in turn, he loved her very much. The fact that they had two daughters and no sons to carry on the family name meant little to him. His branch of the family had inherited the hall from a cousin and he had no real interest in the past glory of the Monmouth name. He would be quite content for Helen and her husband to pass the Hall onto any prospective family they may have. The lack of a male heir, however, bothered my mother very much. As far as she was concerned, it was a failure on their part. She became obsessed with instilling in her daughters the importance of being a good wife and, more importantly, a mother who provided children who were preferably of the right sex. For such an intelligent woman, she was remarkably blinkered about this. We may have grown up during the twentieth century, but we were still very much the product of Victorian values.

As much as Mother was pleased with our intelligence, being decorative and potential wife material was far more important as far as she was concerned. And even more damningly, she firmly believed that the wife who didn't bring babies to a marriage was no wife at all. To be fair to her, society wasn't much different. It was still expected that women would live for the joy of producing offspring and do so within the sanctity of marriage. It had worked like that for centuries, and although women now had the vote, only a few dissenter voices were bothering to question the validity of either at that point. The burning bras brigade were still some years away.

When Helen and Francis married, Mother was in a flutter of excitement. Although the wedding was necessarily low key due to the war, she still made it as special as she could. A Monmouth marriage was something to celebrate. Following the wedding, and whenever she had spare time, she knitted blankets and matinee jackets for the grandchildren she fully expected to arrive without delay.

As the months passed and no grandchild was forthcoming, she found it harder to hide her disappointment. Veiled hints became less veiled and downright to the point. Helen found it unbearable. She longed for a child and was made to feel like a failure, not by her husband but by her own mother. My own tragedy was a diversion that allowed Helen to spend ample time in my room away from Mother's unwelcome words. I may have taken little comfort from my sister's presence in those initial weeks and months, but I am glad my room was a sanctuary for both of us.

A few weeks after I met Robert on the bench by the willow tree, Helen found me in the garden. She was breathless and her eyes sparkled. A new shimmer of beauty seemed to surround her as she clutched my hands and told me it had finally happened. She and Francis were expecting a baby. Although I was elated for her, I quickly suppressed the little flare of jealousy that hit my stomach. My time would come. Helen deserved to enjoy her moment.

Mother was ecstatic when they told her. She moved around the house like a cat with every last drop of the cream. She impressed upon my father the need to refurbish the faded nursery wing. Our old christening gown was unearthed from a trunk and tissue paper. Mary was tasked with preparing special hearty breakfasts each day for Helen to consume under our mother's watchful eye. Fremell Hall was en fête for the bundle of joy which was not due to appear for another seven months.

To do justice to my mother, we were all in a frenzy of excitement. Helen positively glowed, and Francis took the greatest care to ensure her comfort was of paramount importance to everyone else in the house. When Robert and Daddy announced our engagement, my mother's cup was full. One daughter happily married with a much-longed-for baby on the way, and the other daughter thankfully over her emotional episode and engaged to be married to a man of good character. Life was good.

And then, of course, the bubble burst. One night, a furious knocking on my door dragged me from my bed. Shrugging into my dressing gown, I opened the door to see Francis standing there wringing his hands. He looked dreadful. Normally so precise to a pin, he had thrown his clothes on anyhow and his habitually clean-shaven chin was covered with the beginnings of stubble.

"Francis! Whatever's the matter? Oh God, is it Helen?"

"Yes, she's...she's bleeding. You know, down there. I think it's the baby." Francis's natural mortification about talking of women's issues was overborne with a struggle.

"Have you phoned Dr Caldbeck?"

"He's on his way. He wanted someone to sit with her.

Er… I haven't told Elizabeth yet. I thought it might be better if you sat with her instead."

Picturing my mother's inevitable reaction, I couldn't help but agree.

As we hurried along the corridor, I willed everything to be fine. Women had babies all the time. Helen and her baby would be just fine.

When I entered their room, I could tell this wasn't so. Helen lay under a sheet that was practically the same colour as her face. Well, apart from the blood which smeared the area covering her lower half. The contrast was quite shocking, and I gulped down air in an effort to remain calm.

I was no expert, but I could tell this wasn't good. Helen's sobs cut through and I moved to take her hand. Francis gave me a nod and went to wait for the doctor.

"Oh Doris, I'm losing the baby. I know I am. Mother will be so disappointed."

Even in her darkest hour, Helen was thinking of others. I didn't give Mother a second thought; saving Helen was the priority now. I bathed her forehead and wiped the tears from her cheeks. Her lips were taking on a dreadful blue tinge and I was growing more frantic by the second. Where was Dr Caldbeck?

As if on cue, the door opened and in he came. Professional calm swept in with him and he made his way straight to Helen's side. I have little recollection of what went on in that room. Dr Caldbeck, probably sensing how little help I'd be, sent for Mother, who clamped her lips together and assumed command of the *practicalities. I followed instructions issued by both the doctor and Mother, but my mind was numb. What Helen felt, I can only imagine. By the time Dr Caldbeck left the room, it had been returned to an oasis of calm. Of the bloodied nightgown and sheets, there was no sign. All had been superseded by freshly laundered replacements. There were even fresh flowers on the bedside table.*

Banked up on numerous pillows, Helen was pale and exhausted. Francis was banished from the room and even I was not encouraged to linger. Just before I left my sister to our mother's mercies, I heard her say: "Don't worry, darling. You'll have another. You simply must have another." I closed the door on Helen's reply, leant against the door frame and wept.

The next week was hellish. The house was subdued and a replica of the emotional void following Douglas's death. I shudder even now at the memory. Helen blamed herself. She referred to herself as a barren wife and wept bitter tears.

"What if I never have a baby? We've been trying since we were married and now this!"

"Nonsense!" said Mother. "We've never had anything like that in the family. This is just one of those things. The sooner you are intimate with Francis again, the better."

Compassion was never really her thing, but the harshness of her words made an impact on both of us.

As Helen started to recover, physically at least, I reflected on those callous words.

'Nothing like this in the family before.' Yet it was hard to deny that Helen and Francis were hardly fecund. They were

approaching their second wedding anniversary, and this was the first time their hopes had been raised.

Maybe it just wouldn't happen for them. Maybe Fremell Hall was destined to come to my children instead. My heart ached for Helen as I thought of her sorrow coupled with the indignation she'd face from Mother. I can't help but think if Helen and I had been born into a different generation or even a different family, things may have turned out very differently.

I have found recounting this terrible time even more draining than Douglas's death. I must beg your forgiveness for breaking off again, but I must rest.

I'm not certain, obviously, but I can't imagine Helen ever mentioned this to you. Our generation didn't and some would say it's not much different now. Thousands of women will have suffered in silence the way she did. Thousands of women will have just got back on with their lives, not wanting to cause a fuss or draw unwanted attention to themselves. As for Francis, he never talked about it ever again. Well, certainly not to me. As a man who barely believed ladies swore or sweated, the thought of him discussing anything so intimate boggles my mind.

Your mother was frail for some time afterwards and I know Francis was worried that she might lock herself away as I had. You could say it was me who jolted her out of her melancholy and back into the real world, but more of that another time.

All my love
X

CHAPTER 11

Poor Mum! Doris was right. I'd had no idea. She'd never mentioned it to either Susan or me. Losing a child was outside my realm of experience, but the thought of it was devastating. Mum must have been broken-hearted. Poor Dad, he would have carried his pain and loss around with his usual stoicism. Talking about feelings was never his strong point and society certainly didn't encourage men to explore them back then.

In some ways, modern life can seem more stressful than the less complicated times of my youth, but some things have changed for the better. Clive himself had referred more men to counselling and therapy than ever before in the run-up to his retirement. He said it was good they were finally connecting with their emotions. Mum and Dad would just have been left to sink or swim. In a way, both Doris and Helen had been failed by the society of the time.

What an emotional day this was turning into. I'd cried,

gasped with horror and tried to take in so much information I felt it was time for me to take a break as well as Doris. I stretched my legs and my foot knocked into Benji, who immediately jumped up and came to lay his head on my lap. I stroked his ears and he leaned his weight on me.

"Do you know, lad, I think I need something more substantial than a cream cake."

Doris had warned me there was more to come, and I needed sustenance to help me digest it. I crossed the lawn, stepped into the sunroom, and was surprised to find it empty. Neither Clive nor the letters were there, so I guessed he was in his study. I went to check, and yes, the door was pushed to. A sure sign that Clive was immersed deep in something and didn't want to be disturbed.

I returned to the kitchen, opened the fridge and waited for inspiration. It didn't come. The beeps to tell me the door had been open too long brought me back to earth. Right Eve, focus. I grabbed the cheese, salad and butter and dumped them on the worktop. The breadbin held home-made buns, which were a day old but good enough for a slightly distracted lunch. I made enough for Clive too. He'd be in need after reading Doris's revelations.

Benji hovered around my feet. After six years of living with us, he was still unable to remember that he was only allowed to eat dog food or doggy treats.

The 'Forget-me-not' teapot was on the side, so I gave it a quick rinse and left it to drain before taking my lunch to the sunroom. Maybe some time to reflect on all that I'd read would be a good thing. My mind flitted from letter to letter. The fact that Doris was very much alive still blew my mind. All those years thinking she was dead and not even giving her a second thought in my life. Helen and Francis must have had a good reason to keep her existence a secret from me, but I couldn't help but feel cheated. And Doris, too...the fact she'd never attempted to make contact until now was so strange given how determined she seemed.

Thoughts of my grandparents flooded in next. My grandfather, William, had died when I was around fifteen. He was an upright, old-fashioned man who dressed with precision. I'd never seen him in anything other than a suit or at his most relaxed, blazer and slacks. Although not demonstrative, he was devoted to his family. Having us all together around the dining table for Sunday lunch was the highlight of his week. He had always given off an air of faded aristocracy that made sense now I knew about Fremell Hall. I don't remember him ever raising his voice to anyone, yet everyone showed him the utmost respect. Susan and I were always made to feel special.

Grandmother had been a fond grandparent. She'd told us story after story, and she always bought us beautiful books (many of which I still have). She'd spent hours patiently teaching us how to sew and embroider, and her words of encouragement ensured neither of us gave up. Our favourite thing was to go through her jewellery box. We'd drape ourselves in strings of pearls and amber beads. It seemed like a treasure trove to Susan and I. Admittedly, she hadn't been over-generous in the hugs department, but we'd felt loved. There had certainly been no sign of the cold, callous behaviour Doris had referred to.

When Grandpa died, she'd maintained a dignified calm, but she seemed to shrink before our eyes. Her once perfect posture became stooped, almost as if the very prop she needed to remain upright had been pulled away. She turned increasingly to Mary, who still kept house for them. It was Mary who ensured she ate and insisted on still cooking Sunday lunch for us all. This tiny, bird-like woman steered her through those first dreadful months of grieving. Although Grandma lived to see both mine and Susan's children born, she never sparkled in the same way she had when we were small. She must have loved Grandpa far more than Doris imagined. All of this was making me question how well I knew any of my family at all. These letters had changed my perception of everyone and everything I thought I'd known. I had a feeling they would change me too.

I finished the last mouthful of cheese bun and brushed my hands together to get rid of the flour and crumbs. Breaktime was over and I should get back to Doris. I left Clive's lunch covered with a bowl next to the Aga. He'd know to look under there. This was another of our many rituals.

A quick trip to the bathroom and then armed with what felt like my hundredth cup of tea, I padded back across the garden to the sanctuary of the Summer House. Benji, as ever, was at my heels. I stooped to pick up his ball and sent him scurrying across the grass after it.

Once inside the Summer House, I sat down and took

a restorative sip of tea. Benji dropped his ball hopefully at my feet.

"Not now, lad. Lie down."

He seemed to realise I meant it and snuggled back down with his tail just brushing my ankle. I pulled the pile of remaining letters towards me. There was no putting it off any longer....

Letter Number Six

Darling Eve,

Helen's loss affected me in a way that would dramatically change all our lives. My mother's words, 'Nothing like this in the family', continued to prey on my mind. What if Francis and Helen never had a child? What if I were unable to have a child? What would happen to the family home? I'm fairly certain this thought never occurred to my father, but it did to me. As for Mother, she wouldn't have allowed herself to think such a thing was even a possibility.

Two weeks following the miscarriage, Helen was still very weak, and I couldn't see her and Francis even attempting to try for a baby any time soon. It was around then I started to think about my own future with Robert.

He was never going to be, could never be Douglas, but I was very fond of him, and he clearly loved me. It had seemed logical that we would marry and, in the course of time, have children. Helen's experience was forcing me to re-consider. I had to be sure. I had to be certain that conceiving a child was something I could actually do before we married or what was the point?

I know history likes to examine the morals of previous generations and normally, in my experience, cover them with a rose-tinted view. The general belief was that ladies from that time had to be virtuous and marriage was the only way a respectable woman could indulge in sexual activity. Utter rot! Sex has been enjoyed by both sexes outside of marriage since the wedding ceremony first began—a patriarchal event if ever there was one. The history books are littered with babies born on the wrong side of the blanket. Our family personally knew three young ladies of impeccable background who had married in haste and produced 'honeymoon babies'.

Although this hadn't been in my original plan, I was willing to adapt.

Robert had arranged to take a week off work so he could come and support the family in our time of need. Getting Francis out of the house and from under our feet was his chief role. He also made sure I took time away from Helen's side. Even Mother warmed to him, allowing him to take her for a daily turn around the garden. The first day Helen came down to join us, it was Robert who helped Francis carry her downstairs. He was truly becoming part of the family.

Robert and I hadn't actually discussed a date for our wedding, but Mother wouldn't let a little detail like that put her off bringing it up. 'Sooner rather than later' was her suggestion. Robert agreed. He was the type of man who'd do his best to do whatever Mother or I wished. In that respect, he was perfect. The date Mother had in mind was in ten weeks. I hadn't banked on it being quite so soon.

"It will be nice for us to have something to look forward to and it will be good for Helen." Nothing like a bit of emotional blackmail to get everyone on side.

So that was that! The seduction of Robert had a deadline and I had no time to lose. After dinner that evening, I suggested we go for a walk and Robert happily agreed. As usual, our meanderings took us on a loop past the river and 'our bench' and then back to the house. Instead of going to the front door, I pulled Robert towards the path that led off towards the woods.

Halfway along stood our Summer House. It was really rather delightful with a comfy chaise longue, a writing desk with all the usual paraphernalia, a chair and a good quality rug. As we sat on the chaise longue, I reached toward Robert and kissed him. Not a chaste, gentle kiss like the ones we had so far enjoyed but one that held a promise of more to come. Although surprised by the intensity, Robert responded as I had hoped.

"Maybe we could come back here tomorrow evening," I whispered in his ear before leading him back towards the door. He gulped and nodded.

Don't worry, Eve, I won't make you blush with my revelations, but for all that Robert was a gentleman, he was also a man. The following evening, I didn't give him much opportunity to do anything other than follow my lead. Afterwards, we lay sated on the rug, and he stroked my hair. It was the first time I'd felt truly content in a long time. Our evening walks and visits to the Summer House continued for the rest of Robert's stay. And on our final evening, before he left, he told me he couldn't wait for me to be his wife. Now, I just had to wait.

The next month dragged by as far as I was concerned. Helen was healing, well, physically at least, and was taking part in family life again. Mother was knee-deep in wedding dress patterns, talks with the vicar and catering plans. Robert visited when he could and bore all the signs of a man both in love and lust. As for me, I counted the days to see whether my plan had worked.

When more than a month had passed without my usual visit from Mother Nature, I allowed myself to hope. Although Helen was unaware of my situation, I'd never felt more in tune with her. The thought of a little miracle growing inside me left me breathless with joy. No wonder she had looked so radiant.

Robert's next visit was due to take place on the weekend of the Village Dance. I was still undecided whether to write and tell *him I was pregnant before he arrived. After much thought, I decided that reading the news in a letter might be a bit of a shock for him. I am aware of the great irony of that last sentence given how many letters full of varying degrees of shock you have read so far, Eve. In the end, I decided that face to face would be better. By then, I'd be two months pregnant and our wedding just two weeks away. Everything so far was going just as I'd hoped. I should have known by then that fate would have other plans. Between them, Father and Robert ruined everything.*

I must warn you now that the next letter is neither pretty nor my finest hour. Remorse and self-reproach have been my constant companions for many years. Loyally, they have stuck by my side wherever I have gone and whatever I have done. I have faced the realisation that they will be the only things beside me in death. I accept them. I accept my fate.

All my love
X

CHAPTER 13

What on earth had Doris done? And why were Robert and my grandpa the cause of whatever she was guilty of? I re-read the last few lines of the letter and my stomach contracted. Fear tugged at my insides and butterflies flew with nervous energy. What further shocks could Doris have in store for me?

My ordered, stable life was wobbling. Maybe it would be better if the letters had never arrived. Clive and I would have been pottering around the garden keeping the plants in check. Or, we'd have been thinking of taking a run out to the hills or simply watching an old movie. Instead, Clive was shut away in his study, and I was in the Summer House absorbing my new history and trying to come to terms with the fact that my parents had lied to me for most of my life!

As much as I wanted to read the next letter, part of me wanted to pretend it didn't exist. Maybe I could just bury my head and think about what to make for dinner. I glanced at the unopened envelopes. I could simply put them away for another day or even refuse to read them full stop.

Come on, Eve, who are you kidding?

In the house, the telephone rang, and I jumped. I had a choice. Answer it and give myself a much-needed break or ignore it and delve deeper into Doris's world. The ringing stopped and within a minute, Clive appeared at the sunroom door—decision made it seemed. I crossed the grass with Benji at my heels.

"It's Susan. I wasn't sure if you wanted to speak to her, so I told a little white lie. I said you were in the shower and I'd see if you were finished. Do you want to speak to her?"

My sister Susan. Oh God, did I want to speak to her? I looked at Clive, who was calmly waiting for my response.

"Can you tell her I'll ring her later? I just can't bring myself to talk to her at the moment."

"Of course, love. I'll let her know." Clive reached out a hand and ran a gnarled finger down my cheek. Tears filled my eyes and spilled over. His fingertip caught them and he pulled me close.

As ever, Benji objected to any display of affection that didn't involve him. He jumped up, but we ignored him, and I clung to Clive like my life depended on him. Only when Benji added his voice to his objections did we pull apart.

"Eve, everything will be ok. I'd best get back to Susan."

Clive's departure left me feeling bereft. I groped blindly for the box of tissues on the sunroom table. I blew my nose and felt a little better. Deciding that I might need more hankies to mop up my tears, I tucked the box under my arm and stepped back out into the garden.

The impact of all these revelations would affect Susan too. She had a right to know the full story, but not until I knew what that actually was and had had time to digest it all. It might be easier to simply give her the letters as I had with Clive. But that decision would have to wait for another day. As much as I loved her, I simply couldn't face bursting her bubble just yet.

The sun was fully on the Summer House now. The light rays showed the dust motes dancing in their beams. I passed through them into Doris's world.

I sat down, settled Benji at my feet and pulled the next letter towards me.

Letter Number Seven

Dearest Eve,

When I first decided to write to you after all these years, I knew my letters would come as a bolt out of the blue. It was obvious you hadn't wanted to make contact over the intervening years, and although this had hurt me, I'd accepted it as yet another part of my lot.

I also knew that this letter would be the hardest for me to write and for you to read. I'm not a bad person, Eve. Used to my own way, spoilt, headstrong and a little wayward maybe, but I would never have thought of myself as bad. I just happen to be a person who ended up doing a terrible thing. I hope you can remember that as this letter unfolds.

The weekend of the Village Dance had arrived and so had Robert. This would be the last time he'd visit before the wedding and we had some last-minute plans to confirm. Mother was at her most benign, and she welcomed Robert with genuine warmth and bestowed appraising but satisfied glances upon mine and Helen's dress choices for the evening.

As ever on these occasions, we were enjoying an early dinner before strolling to the Village Hall. The weather was warm, and although not bright, the hazy sunshine was nice enough to pass for a summer's day in August.

During dinner, I could tell Father had an announcement to make. He kept fiddling with his tie and exchanging glances with Mother. It came as no surprise to me when he thanked Mary for dinner then told her to take herself off to the dance once the clearing up was done.

"Take yourself off for a twirl, Mary," is how he put it.

She never ever did, but she smiled and replied as always, "Thank you, sir. That would be lovely."

As Mary left the room, Father stretched out and squeezed my hand before addressing the room.

His words were highly complimentary to myself and warmly welcoming to Robert, who he referred to as another son joining the family. He couldn't be more delighted that his darling daughter had found love with a man like him. Robert blushed and looked uncomfortable. Father ended his speech by formally offering us a home at Fremell Hall following our marriage. The family would be complete, he said. He and Mother would be delighted to have both their daughters and respective husbands under one happy and united roof.

I can't say this surprised me. Francis had made his home here once he'd tied the knot with Helen. His family lived in Essex with numerous siblings needing accommodation in their comfortable but by no means large house. As a younger brother, he had been only too happy to exchange his busy and chaotic family home for the more tranquil setting at Fremell Hall. I'd just assumed that Robert, with no family home left and a house with no attachments in the Welsh Borders, would have been happy to do the same. Glancing at him, I could see he looked quite startled. It dawned on me that we hadn't actually discussed where we would live once our marriage vows were exchanged. This was clearly something we'd have to address. I had no doubt I'd bring Robert around to mine and Father's way of thinking.

For now, though, it was time to make our way to the dance. Robert was quiet and distant. His usual conversation and telling me I looked beautiful was missing. I asked him if anything was amiss, but he said we'd discuss it later when we were back from the dance. The walk to the village seemed longer than usual, but eventually, the ever-present fluttering bunting heralded our arrival. It wouldn't surprise me if it's still there to this day. The bunting continued up the path and over the entrance to the hall, and the music and community engulfed us as we stepped inside. Dresses of every colour swirled and twirled around the room, and those who weren't dancing were engaged in animated conversation. Francis led Helen onto the dance floor and she looked like her old self for the first time in weeks.

While Robert accompanied Father to order drinks, I found myself accosted by Douglas's former love interest Margaret Holland—well, Margaret Fallows as she now was. We were always icily civil and generally muttered a few pleasantries before moving on, duty done. Tonight, she congratulated me on my forthcoming marriage.

"Such a relief for you after losing Douglas and with so few men around to choose from. Lucky for me, I'd already married Reg, or you might have got in first!" Her smile couldn't disguise the venom in her eyes and I was in no mood for her petty remarks.

For once, I didn't even bother to respond—typical Margaret talking about Douglas when I'm at a dance with Robert. Speaking of whom, I was worried about him. He just didn't seem himself. For some reason, Father's words had made him withdrawn and remote. Although we danced and joined conversations, I felt as if we were in different places all night. I just couldn't get close to him and I couldn't wait to make an excuse and leave.

Eventually, my wish was granted. I slipped my hand through the crook of his arm, and we made our way back. The silence was suffocating. Three times I attempted conversation, and three times I was ignored. In the end, with my temper rising, I fell silent. Not the silence of acquiescence but the silence of smouldering rage. No man had ever ignored me before and if Robert thought this would be something I'd endure after we married, he could jolly well think again.

As the gates came into view, I tugged at Robert's arm, and we made our way to the Summer House, not that either of us had romance on our minds. I leant against the desk while Robert settled himself on the edge of the chaise longue. I have replayed this scene a thousand times or more over the years. I can even recall the knotholes on the ceiling beams. Everything is imprinted on my mind, so I will recount it as it happened.

"Robert, talk to me. What on earth's the matter? You've barely said two words all night and I will NOT be ignored."

"Doris, I didn't mean to ignore you. I'm just trying to put my thoughts into words. I don't want you to think I'm ungrateful. Your parents' offer is incredibly generous. It's just not where I imagined living once we were married."

"Well, where do you imagine living then? We've not talked about this at all."

"It sounds as if you just presumed we would stay here. How long for Doris? Until your parents die? Until we are old ourselves? It never occurred to me that you'd want to stay here."

"And what's wrong with here? It's a perfectly lovely house. Just where did you think I would find acceptable after here?" I was starting to get really cross. Why was he being so awkward?

"I've got a house ready for us. It's not far from where I live now. I was keeping it as a surprise so it would be a wedding gift for

you. It's a lovely place, Doris. It might not be as big and grand as this, but it's perfect for us and any family we may have."

Instinctively, my hand moved to my, for now, flat stomach. I still hadn't told him.

"I wanted somewhere just for us. I really think you'll love it, Doris. I don't want to offend your family. I was hoping you'd be pleased and when we told them about our new house, they'd see how enthusiastic you were about it and be happy for us. Give us their blessing."

A new home far away on the Welsh Borders. Many girls would have jumped at the chance, but my life was sewn into the fabric of the walls of Fremell Hall. I couldn't imagine living anywhere else, and more importantly, I didn't want to imagine living anywhere else.

"You should have told me. How on earth can I wax lyrical about a house I've never seen and know nothing about? You've never mentioned it before. You've just presumed I'll be happy to move."

"Be fair, Doris, I could say the same. It's a man's job to provide a home for his wife. I don't want to rely on your parents. You and your family have just assumed we'd be staying here. It's very unusual for a woman not to move into their husband's home, you know."

"Well, maybe the Monmouths aren't usual then! What's wrong with living here anyway? It's my home."

"I'm not saying there's anything wrong with it. It's a beautiful house, but I'm simply saying I'd rather provide for my wife instead. Do you understand?"

I didn't know what to understand. My easy-going fiancé was rapidly changing into a stubborn schoolboy, which was not a transformation I was happy with. As I looked at him, it dawned on me that I categorically did not want to leave Fremell Hall. I didn't want our child, my child, to be born in a house that wasn't mine. My child would be born here just as Helen and I had been. And, if Helen and Francis didn't have any children, my child would make sure the Hall remained in the family.

"I don't want to move, Robert. This is my home and I want to share it with you."

"But that's the point. It's not just yours, is it? We'd be sharing with William and Elizabeth and Francis and Helen. We'd have no privacy, no time just for us. I can't understand you, Doris. I thought you'd be pleased." Robert looked hurt, but I was too wrapped up in my annoyance to care.

"Pleased! Pleased that you're uprooting me and making me move to the other side of the country?" My temper was really starting to bubble.

"Oh, come on, it's hardly the ends of the earth." Robert was starting to get annoyed too.

"I can't leave Helen. She needs me." I was clutching at emotional straws with both hands.

"Helen will be just fine. She has her husband to look after her. Remember, that's what husbands are supposed to do."

"Robert, I really don't want to move. You should have told me instead of just springing this on me." I unleashed the tears from my arsenal.

"I realise that now. But honestly Doris, the house is lovely, and I'm sure you'll like it. Won't you at least come and see it? You'll see how happy we could be there."

Unusually, my tears had failed, and he remained completely unmoved. Why was he being so stubborn? Normally he just gave me whatever I asked for. It was clearly time to up the ante.

"Even if I do come and see it, it won't change anything. I want our children to be born here, just like I was."

"Doris, I think you are being a little unreasonable. You know I want you to have everything you desire, but I thought this would make you happy. Can't you just consider it for me?"

"I can't, Robert. My life is here. My memories are here."

"Memories. At last, we're getting to the real reason. I can't help thinking that if Douglas were the one asking, your answer would be very different."

"How dare you! You have no right to mention his name. No right to bring him into this argument. How could you?" My tears were full of rage now and I dashed them off my cheeks like bullets.

"Well, it's true, isn't it? The sainted Douglas could have asked you to go to the moon and you'd have gone." I pushed myself away from the desk and stepped forward. Robert stood up and held out his hands. *"Doris, Doris, my love, I'm sorry. I'm so sorry. It was unforgivable of me to mention him. But you do have to get over him, or I'm only ever going to be second best. I'm here; Douglas is dead. You have to accept that."*

"I have accepted it. I've accepted you, haven't I? I'm marrying you. If I hadn't got over him, I'd have joined a convent or something equally hideous. Just because I don't want to leave here doesn't mean I'm not over him." I was icy with fury.

"Doesn't it? I think you won't leave here because this is where you met him. For God's sake, Doris, the man is dead!" Those eight simple words were his undoing.

I flew at him. I wanted to shake him into submission and punish him for bringing Douglas into the room. He put out his hands instinctively and we grappled in an inelegant, breathless and furious kind of waltz. Robert tried to contain my flailing hands and arms while I tried just as hard to hit out at him.

Our terrible choreography took us from the desk towards the chaise longue. Throughout all this, Robert had been trying to reason with me. He kept telling me to be rational and to calm down. Of course, it only made things worse. I was beyond furious.

As we swayed, my heel caught in the rug, which had become rucked up beneath our feet. I fell into Robert and he was caught off guard. He staggered back, and seeing my advantage, I pushed him as hard as I could, and he fell. His head cracked sickeningly on the curved arm of the chaise longue and he slumped to the floor. He was motionless while blood trickled from one ear.

What had I done? Dear God, what had I done?

I knelt by his side and ran my fingers around the back of his head. They came away crimson.

"Robert, Robert! Can you hear me? Oh God, can you hear me?"

Silence.

I sat like a statue, unable to comprehend what had just happened. I honestly think I would have sat there for eternity if Helen's gasp hadn't brought me back to reality. I looked up at her and Francis, and their horrified gaze drowned me.

Unable to bear Helen's disbelief, I returned my gaze to the floor. Robert's blood covered my fingers and his unseeing eyes were fixed on the ceiling. I shuddered.

"It was an accident," I mumbled. "Please help me."

They did, of course. What else could they do? We were family and family stuck together.

That one terrible act changed the course of all our histories. If Douglas hadn't died, if Daddy hadn't presumed we'd remain at Fremell Hall, if Robert hadn't assumed I would move. If, if, if.

Such a small word, but you can beat yourself to flinders with it. A word and sentiment as pointless as preventing ageing. What was done was done. What was past was past. What was gone was gone. Douglas was gone, Robert was gone, and now I was a killer. It seems strange to write that statement in black and white. I never imagined I'd have to write to my daughter telling her I'd killed her father, but it's true, Eve. Robert was dead and at my *hands. Like Lady Macbeth, I've tried to wash away his blood, but it remains to this day.*

I'm so sorry to stop again, Eve. I'm utterly exhausted, physically and emotionally. Yet there is still so much to say.

I'm so sorry,
D x

CHAPTER 15

"No! Dear God, NO!" The words tore from me and Doris's letter fell from my fingers.

A murderer. The word bounced off the wooden walls and attacked me from every angle. I shuddered and found myself on my feet, pacing the Summer House floor. Recalling what Doris had done in hers, I shuddered again and felt an overwhelming urge to get out.

I stumbled into the garden swallowing down bile and breathing hard. Benji whined and leant against my leg, but I ignored him. I strode to the flower bed on the opposite side of the garden. The little hand fork was propped up against the fence from Clive's weeding earlier this morning. Before I knew it, the fork was in my hands, and I was kneeling by the flower bed, jabbing viciously at the soil. The anger which had been carefully controlled for so many years exploded from me. Stab, stab, stab. I attacked the ground and turned over the soil, nearly dismembering one of my favourite plants. Benji kept his distance.

After ten minutes, I was exhausted. I dropped the fork and I sat back on my heels. I steadied myself with my hands that shook. I had never felt so close to fainting. I desperately tried to squash the jumble of thoughts in my head. Our own Summer House seemed to loom over me as a dreadful reminder; a Grim Reaper in maple and furniture. I couldn't even look at the place we'd always regarded as our little piece of heaven. Our sanctuary from everyday life was no longer somewhere I wanted to be. The crime may not have been committed there, but it screamed death!

Easing myself upright, I knew I had to go back inside it. I took a shaky breath, stepped over the threshold and hastily collected the letters from the table. I pulled the door to behind me and hurried to the house. As I stepped into the sunroom, I tried to decide if I wanted a drink. Was it too early for gin? I dumped the letters on the little table and headed to the kitchen. The first thing that greeted me was the teapot upside down on the draining board. Its beautiful lines and nod to times gone by mocked me. Another wave of rage came from nowhere and the teapot was in my hands. Before I knew it, it was smashed all over the floor.

"Eve, what was that?" Clive's voice came anxiously from along the hallway.

Somehow, I was on the kitchen floor sobbing hysterically. Pieces of china made an island of me, and I desperately needed saving. Clive's head appeared, and the trained doctor in him assessed the situation. He shut Benji and his vulnerable paws in the sunroom, then turned to me.

"Eve, are you all right?" I gulped and looked up at my life raft. The relief washed over me when I felt his hands on mine. "Come on, up you get."

Somehow, in an ungainly stiff-limbed manoeuvre, he got me upright where I collapsed into his arms and wept unrestrainedly. Clive patted and soothed and uttered meaningless platitudes of comfort and hope. After a few minutes, my tears stopped and inevitably, my nose started to run. Once again, Clive stepped in with his crisp, clean hankie.

"Eve, what's happened now? Is it Doris?"

I nodded, trying to find the right words.

"Clive, it's just awful...she...she...." I couldn't bring myself to finish.

"Go into the sunroom. I'll bring you a cup of tea."

"No!" I practically shrieked. "No more bloody tea. I want a brandy, a large brandy."

Clive didn't even question it and turned to the drinks' cabinet. Benji's indignation at being shut inside the sunroom had reached a vocal high which stopped as soon as I opened the door and let myself in. I slumped into my trusty chair and gripped the arms with ice-cold hands. Benji's rough tongue ran eagerly over the salty taste. Normally I'd have pushed him away, but I was beyond caring. This latest revelation had shocked me to my core. I hadn't anticipated it, and I was woefully ill-prepared. But can anyone ever be prepared to find out their mother had killed their father?

Clive returned with two glasses sloshing with brandy. My hand shook as I accepted one gratefully. Taking a generous mouthful, I rested my head against the back of the chair and let the liquid warmth flood through me. Clive sat forward, cradling his glass between cupped hands. He wore his best bedside manner face.

"Eve, what's happened now?"

"Have you finished the letters I gave you?"

"Just a couple to go. I can see why you were upset earlier. It's a lot to take in."

"You think that was a lot. Ha!" A bitter laugh escaped. Clive waited with his customary patience. God, it was maddening. I wanted to shake him out of his serenity, to get some kind of emotional reaction. How could he just sit there so calmly?

"Here, you'd better have this one too." I thrust the latest thorn in my side at him. I tossed back the rest of the brandy. "I just want this hideous day to be over. In fact, I'd like to go back to the start of the day and throw Doris's package in the bin."

"Well, that can't happen, sweetheart. You have to accept what has happened and try to stay calm."

"Calm! Yes, right, that's exactly what I need to be told at the moment. I'm not one of your patients, Clive. I'm your wife, and I need to feel cross and angry and really bloody upset. And even more importantly, I need you to listen to me being cross and angry and really bloody upset without telling me to be bloody calm. Oh, just go back to your bloody office, can't you? You're about as useful as a chocolate teapot. Sometimes I wonder why I married you."

I gasped. This was hardly Clive's fault. Breaking teapots and screeching at my husband wasn't going to help. I'd successfully learnt to subdue my temper and keep it under control and its reappearance terrified me. Maybe there was more of Doris in me than I realised. I pushed that thought away quickly.

"I'm sorry, darling, I just don't know what to do or think at the moment."

Clive squeezed my hand and we sat in companionable silence for some time. My outburst was forgotten. But Doris was not. As much as I didn't want to face what she'd done, I had to process it and accept it. I'd also have to see what else she'd written.

As if reading my mind, Clive released my hand, pushed his hair back and asked, "Are you going back outside to read the rest?"

"Dear God, no!" Clive raised his eyebrow at me. "You might not be so keen on the Summer House once you've heard what Doris has to say either. I'll read the rest in here. There's only a few left and surely the worst has been said now."

"She really did put the cat among the pigeons then. Can I take the next few letters I haven't read yet?"

I nodded. Clive finished his brandy and sorted through the letters on the table, leaving me the remaining envelopes. He gave me a reassuring smile and headed back towards his study.

Cat among the pigeons! More like a bloody great tiger, I thought, as I pulled the last few envelopes toward me. I really hoped Doris had no more revelations for me, I wasn't sure how much I could take. I steeled myself. Come on, Eve, better get on with it.

Letter Number Eight

My Darling Eve,

I'm sure my previous letter upset you greatly; it's not every day you receive news like that. I realise it ended quite abruptly and with a really quite shocking disclosure. However, I worded it, and believe me, I started that letter several times, I can't get away from the fact that I killed Robert.

The real tragedy is that I had actually come to love him. It wasn't the all-consuming passion I'd had for Douglas, of course. Even now, that is something I have never forgotten, but I had come to love Robert. The fact that he was attractive, kind, and a decent person made it so much easier for me to fall for him. He was a good man, Eve, and he loved me, was devoted to me. Undoubtedly, he would have loved you too had I given him the chance.

I'll never forget that night. As much as I was determined to have my own way over our living arrangements, I'd never anticipated the outcome that I was left to deal with. Who could have imagined that a simple argument could cause so much damage? When Robert fell to the floor, it was as if I were watching a movie or a play as a mere spectator, not as a proper all singing and dancing actor. I knew straight away he was dead. There was something so final about the way he just lay there. The trickle of blood oozing out from his ear has stayed with me. I reached out to touch it with my fingers. My stomach heaved. I put my ear to his chest, but I already knew I was alone.

Into this walked Helen and Francis. I was totally unaware at first. My attention was wholly on Robert. Helen's gasp brought me back into the here and now. While I've never forgotten the words Robert and I exchanged, the memories of what Helen said have gone. Somehow, they must have dragged the sorry story out of me. I do remember that once they'd established that Robert hadn't simply tripped, but my lamentable temper had had something to do with it, they found it hard to disguise their feelings. Their words may not have stayed with me, but the looks on their faces have. It's the only time Helen looked at me with the eyes of a stranger. Francis's look of utter disbelief tinged with disgust washed over me and I lowered my eyes. Helen eased her way around the rug and sank into the comfy chair. A chair more used to sunset cocktails or pre-dinner aperitifs than murder. She looked shell shocked. Francis came into his own and took over the proceedings.

We had two priorities: to do something with Robert (it seems so callous to write 'body') and to make sure everything in the Summer House was tidy. Francis disappeared, leaving strict instructions for Helen and me to stay there and stay quiet. That wasn't hard to obey. What could we possibly talk about with Robert lying on the floor in front of us? After what seemed like a lifetime, Francis returned with one of the gardener's wheelbarrows which we managed to get Robert into. The farcical nature of our movements only served to add to the horror. It was undignified, unpleasant and thoroughly unworthy of the man I should have been marrying in two weeks' time. I have never asked where he was taken, and Francis never told me. The less I knew, the better was his maxim. There was a quarry in the grounds of Fremell Hall and I have often wondered if that is where poor Robert's final resting place is.

While Francis undertook his grisly job, he ordered Helen and I back to the house for a pail of soapy water. Thankfully the amount of blood to get rid of was minimal but get rid of it, we must.

As soon as Francis had left with Robert, I urged Helen to stay in the chair. She was only too willing to agree. I flitted down the Summer House steps and darted quickly up the path and through the back kitchen entrance. Inevitably, Mary was there making hot milk, and of course, she had the whole sorry story out of me in no *time. Ever supportive, she swallowed whatever shock she had and sprang to action with practical help. Helen and I were her darlings and she'd do anything to help us. Mary would fill the bucket of water while I was to gather Robert's clothes and belongings.*

I didn't even question why but crept up the servants' stairs and along the corridor to Robert's room. The enormity of the evening's events struck me as I gathered up the clothes of a man who would no longer wear them. They still retained his scent and as clichéd as it sounds, I lifted a shirt to my face and inhaled. There was no time for sentimentality, though, and I grabbed his case and practically threw his things inside. Keeping them neat was no longer a necessity.

Back in the kitchen, Mary had the bucket ready. She told me to give Robert's case to Francis to dispose of while the Summer House was tidied. I did wonder if she'd offer to come with me, but she said something about providing an alibi. She asked me to send Francis to her before he went to bed and sat back down at the table to drink her hot milk.

I struggled down the path in my dainty shoes and pretty dress like an out of kilter milkmaid. The case, which I held tightly in one hand, banged into my left knee while the water sloshed around the rim of the bucket, I held just as tightly in my other hand. From time to time, a liberal shower of water drenched my feet and legs. I was glad when the Summer House came into sight.

To avoid our dresses being ruined by the clean-up operation, Helen and I stripped to our petticoats and set to work. Helen, of course, was still recovering from losing the baby, so I did the lion's share, which seemed only fair given the circumstances. It was only once the scrubbing brush was in my hands that my emotions took over. The salty tears, blood and soap mingled in a pink froth that looked like meringue peaks. I have never been able to tolerate rugs in the places I have lived since that evening. The very pattern of that one is emblazoned on the insides of my eyes. I still see it now, both with and without Robert's blood.

The scrubbing brush seemed to free Helen's voice as well. Contempt and disbelief dripped from her words as quickly as my tears dripped into the suds. For some reason, although her final sentence was fairly innocuous, it was the one that hit the hardest.

"I suggest you ask Daddy to re-decorate the Summer House."

With that, she dried her hands, pulled her dress back over her head and sat on the chair like a regal statue. By the time Francis arrived back with the empty barrow, the rug was as clean as it was going to be, and the water had been discarded in the woods. There we sat, the magnificent Monmouths, immaculate in our beautiful dresses in stony silence.

"You do realise we'll have to tell William and Elizabeth," Francis announced as he put his hand protectively on Helen's shoulder.

I jumped. I simply hadn't thought about all of the implications for the situation. Mother and Father would stand by me. I knew they would. The threat of scandal would have had them scurrying to clean the blood themselves. I'd have to face them tomorrow, but now I was suddenly incredibly tired. I gave Francis the case and explained he was to dispose of it. It was Mary's idea, and he was to go and see her in the kitchen once he'd finished. He was beyond questioning anything and simply took the case and left. As one and with no further words, Helen and I left the Summer

House, negotiated the path, let ourselves silently into the house and crept to our respective rooms. Helen didn't even kiss me goodnight.

The breakfast table was not a happy place the following morning. When Robert hadn't appeared, I had to come clean to Mother and Father under the watchful eye of Helen and Francis.

They were incredulous, sickened that any child of theirs could be involved in such an act. They simply couldn't understand how it had happened. I didn't need their understanding, though. I needed their help and of course, they stepped up to the plate magnificently. That's right! Your very respectable grandma and grandpa helped cover up a murder to protect the family name.

Mary's plan had been simple but effective. By disposing of Robert's belongings as well as himself, we could play the part of shocked and bewildered relatives. I started with a worried phone call to his office, who, not surprisingly, hadn't seen him. Daddy phoned Robert's solicitor, who recommended Daddy phone the police to report him missing. When they came knocking at the door a few days later, our story was straight. According to us, Robert had left early Sunday morning and we hadn't seen or heard from him since. Old and respected families can still pull a few strings in the modern world, but back then, this was even more the case. Daddy's old friend, who was something high up in policing, following hints from us, had directed the search towards the Welsh Borders. Who on earth would suspect the Monmouths or the beautiful but tragically bereft wife to be?

Somehow, we'd got away with it. An official missing person file had been opened and the day of the wedding came and went. Cards and flowers from well-wishers (read the insufferably nosy) arrived daily at the house. I could just imagine the lurid gossip. Losing one fiancé was tragic; losing another was bordering on *carelessness. Unable to bear it, I retreated to my room for two days. Whereas last time I had been surrounded by offers of love and support, this time, the family left me alone. Mother came to talk to me once, but it turned into a tirade about my callous nature, my unbelievable selfishness and my unnatural behaviour. In turn, I told her that her stupid obsession with carrying on the family name and ensuring the house stayed in the family had contributed to it. It was an ugly meeting full of ugly words and sentiments. It left both of us emotionally battered.*

Like last time, it was Mary who brought my meals, and I was so grateful for her unquestioning love. I'm sure my behaviour must have horrified her, but she never once made any judgement or comment. Part of me wished I could stay in my room with Mary bringing my food indefinitely. But the music had to be faced.

The first day I ventured back downstairs, the atmosphere was incredibly tense. Mother barely looked at me and Father looked as though I were a total stranger to him. Helen found it hard to be in the same room as me. Funnily enough, it was Francis who tried to make me feel human again. He wasn't exactly gushing with warmth, but he did at least speak to me as if I were a normal person. I'm glad he was the person you knew as your father. He was a good man, Eve.

That evening, Father told me that the family had decided it were best if I leave Fremell Hall and try to make a new life somewhere else. They simply couldn't share the house with me any longer. Surely I must understand. My 'behaviour' as father always referred to the murder as, was shocking and completely unacceptable. They had stood by me and helped cover up, but that was as far as it would go. Robert's will had left me well provided for despite the lack of marriage lines. He'd simply left all his worldly goods to Doris Parr (nee Monmouth)—that simple bracket made all the difference.

There was no need for me to remain in the family home. In fact, it would be better for everyone if I didn't.

Helen was crying. Silent sobs shook her shoulders and caused her to grip her hands tightly together on her lap. Mother was white-faced and even she looked as if she were holding back a tear. So this was it, was it? The dismissal. The family's shameful secret to be set free and cast out. Dear old Daddy. He thought I'd have to bow to their decision about my future. He thought he'd dropped a bombshell that would make me toe the line. Little did he know I had a bombshell of my own—you.

I remember standing up and addressing them as if I were opening Parliament. I explained that yes, of course, I understood their position and embarrassment. I understood they would rather I didn't remain at the Hall, or my home as I prefer to think of it. I was quite prepared to do as they'd asked, but there was one little question I had for them. Were they prepared for their first grandchild to be born on the other side of the country and never see them? As I made my way towards the door, I saw Mother half stand before slumping back into her chair. I'd made my point. No doubt we'd talk about it over dinner.

I appreciate this wasn't the way my parents anticipated receiving news of their first grandchild, but they had forced the time and setting upon me, and cloth must be cut accordingly.

And I must rest accordingly, too. Each letter tires me more than the last. My brain and hand seem less connected than when I wrote the first one. I will write more tomorrow.

All my love
X

CHAPTER 17

Poor Robert! The man I would never truly think of as Dad had surely deserved better than that. There was something cruelly comic about his final scene in the Summer House. Being bundled into a wheelbarrow of all things seemed like a final insult. It was all so mundane and, as Doris herself had said, undignified.

While it was difficult for me to imagine my birth mother as a killer, it was nigh on impossible to imagine my parents and grandparents covering it all up for her. These wonderful, caring people had shaped and moulded my life. They had shown me such love and support. More importantly, they were people I had greatly respected and looked up to. How could they be involved in something like this? On the other hand, they'd lied to me for years and told me Doris was dead. How little I knew them! And how little I knew Mary! She had been part of our childhood and her wholesome soups and scones were the first things Susan and I had learnt to cook. Tiny, bird-like Mary who had cared for our grandmother and held her together after Grandpa died, the mastermind of the cover-up. If someone had told me she was a secret lion tamer, I couldn't have been more surprised.

I became aware of the sun shining in through the window. The brandy had soothed and calmed me initially, but it had left me with a parched throat. I needed a drink and definitely not tea! I heaved myself from the chair with limbs that seemed weighed down by Doris's letters and made my way to the kitchen. Clive had shifted the remnants of the teapot onto a piece of newspaper and the draining rack was empty. I was starting to regret my spurt of temper. I looked at the jagged pieces and ruined pattern. I'd done a very thorough job. The spout had been broken off and the main body of the pot was split into three. Various chips were missing from the rim and the base; there would be no chance of putting it back together. It was beyond repair, just like Robert. It's always so hard to know what to do with broken crockery, nobody seems to want it and you can't just sling it in the bin. The teapot had been part of our lives since the day we married. It may be broken, but I couldn't quite bring myself to discard it. I had no idea what I could possibly do with it, maybe a craft project with one of the grandchildren or a mosaic planter for the garden. Either way, I knew for certain I had to keep hold of the pieces. It could stay on the newspaper for now; its fate could be decided another time. Funnily enough, the lid was absolutely perfect, not a blemish on it. I ran my fingers over the smooth surface. The gilt was as shiny as the day we received it and the pattern delicate but finely drawn— what a contrast to the damaged body.

I tried to push the thought of the broken teapot and

the broken man from my mind, took a glass out of the cupboard and turned on the tap. I trailed my fingers through the water until it ran cold. My glass filled and overflowed as the image of Robert lying dead on the rug forced its way back inside my head. Benji barked and I became aware of the water spilling down the drain.

"Let's find you a treat, shall we, lad?"

Benji's nose was on high alert as I pulled open his snack drawer and fished out his favourite disgusting smelling snacklet. He took it gently from my fingers and carried his prize away to his bed. I wasn't ready to join him in the sunroom just yet. I needed time to think.

In a few short hours, Doris's letters had turned my world upside down. I no longer felt like Eve Gilchrist, daughter of Francis and Helen Fenwick. Now I had become daughter of Doris Monmouth – killer, and Robert Parr – victim. I shuddered. How could this be happening to me?

I remember conversing with friends once about how normal and every day I was, how I longed for a bit of drama or excitement to liven life up a bit. They'd laughed and told me I'd never be able to handle it. They were right. I didn't want to handle it. A life less ordinary was not for me after all. Safe, dependable, regular and full of good sense. That's how I was regarded. Some people probably thought I was a little dull or boring, but that was ok. I knew that the words people used to describe me were an accurate reflection. We couldn't all be trailblazers and adventure seekers. But now it seemed I had a new adjective—Bombshell.

This is a word that conjures up images of Hollywood glamour. Film starlets, gorgeous clothes, furs, knock 'em dead fashion and looks. Although I can look back on my younger self and acknowledge I was a very pretty girl, I was never and would never be Bombshell material. But of course, that wasn't what Doris had meant. I was the Bombshell to shatter the tranquillity of William and Elizabeth's plans to keep tight control of Doris, get her out of Fremell Hall and away from the village speculation. The Bombshell who would devastate the family's good name. The Bombshell born out of wedlock who would plunge the Monmouth name into shame. I'd never been so exciting or interesting in my life!

Was I the reason they'd left Fremell Hall? Had the shame been too much and the gossip unbearable? But that couldn't be so. We'd stayed at the Hall until I was about five. And at what point had Helen and Francis adopted me? There were still so many unanswered questions, and I had no guarantee that Doris would answer them all for me.

The only thing I knew with any certainty was that Doris had killed Robert, and my dad Francis had gone to his grave without revealing where the body was. How on earth had a sentence like that become my reality?

I drained my glass of water and refilled it once more. I didn't want to delay any longer. It was time to return to my history.

Letter Number Nine

Darling Eve,

Firstly, my apologies; my concentration is getting worse and worse. I didn't realise how long it would take to write this all down for you. It's hard to be brief and to the point when you are recounting such an epic part of your life's history and one that took place so long ago. You'll be glad to know the worst of the shocks are over. My confessions will be less difficult for you to read and understand from now on.

After I'd made my dramatic announcement, I retired to my room. I needed to formulate my words and thoughts, ready for the inevitable crossfire at dinner. For once, the amount of starch used on the napkins would not be Mother's priority.

I made a special effort with my dress and hair and presented myself at cocktail hour. There was none of this 'no drinking while pregnant' directive back then, and I needed a steadier. While Mary bustled around with a tray of glasses, we maintained a quiet air of calm. Not that there was anything we could keep from Mary. Afterall, she was the instigator of our cover-up story and would undoubtedly be involved in any future plans we made. But we all like to fool ourselves that we're in control, so it was business as usual and a dignified calm to cover it all. Underneath the tastefully decorated and civilised room, though, a storm was on its way. As soon as Mary had closed the door behind her, Mother turned to me and uttered one word.

"Well?"

Well, Eve, I let her have it. I was not going to be shuffled off out of the way. I wanted my baby to be born and brought up at Fremell Hall. Surely, we could all live together amicably? Surely this was a better solution than banishing me? And besides, there was no telling what I might do or say if I wasn't under their eye. Mother was furious.

"How on earth do you expect us to let you have the baby here? The gossip, the slander, the common people from the village all speculating, I can't bear the thought of it. It's bad enough facing all the gossip now. People are wondering if Robert has run off because he didn't want to marry you. There's even talk of another woman. It's humiliating, Doris!"

"I'm quite aware of the humiliation, Mother. Do you think I relish being an object of pity and rampant curiosity?"

As ever, Father stepped in. He promised us a solution that would please everyone as much as possible in this situation. But first, he needed to speak to Helen. Helen looked up quickly and he beckoned her over. Together, they slipped through the doors onto the terrace.

Mother, Francis and I remained silent on the inside. We didn't even drink. We simply stood clutching our glasses and watched as Helen and Father walked first to one end of the terrace and then back. They did this several times. Once Helen cried out and shot a look towards us all. My father steadied her and they continued walking. Finally, she turned to Father and nodded. She gave him a brief kiss on the cheek and he patted her shoulder before opening the door for them both. Their re-entry broke the spell, and we drank in unison like synchronised swimmers coming up for air.

The plan was really quite simple. Another of Daddy's old friends had a second home in the South of France. We'd holidayed there on several occasions. Old Jonty was always offering it to us for a longer-term visit, and this would be the perfect time to accept.

We'd travel there en masse; Mother, Father, Helen, Francis and of course me. Mary would come too. For the next eight months or so, we'd live there, far away from the prying eyes of the village. And when we finally did return, who was to think that the baby belonged to anyone else other than Helen and Francis? The locals would be delighted that the lovely couple who so longed for a child had been granted a blessing. The child would be theirs, brought up as theirs and I would still be able to see the baby grow. Father felt it was the perfect solution. Mother was happy to clutch at any straws to save face and Helen had only to talk to Francis, whose devotion was never going to get in the way of her happiness. As for me, I'd have to accept that my child wouldn't be born at Fremell Hall. And the other stipulations? I was sure they could be adapted in my favour once you arrived, so I agreed as well.

I won't bore you with the details and logistics of it all. Needless to say, Daddy arranged everything, and with Mother on board to assist him, the outcome could only ever be as they wished. We notified the police of our plans and urged them to get in touch without delay if Robert contacted them. Mary bustled around packing, sorting and covering furniture with sheets. Within no time at all, the Hall was shut up and we were on our way.

Jonty's house was a charming villa with a wonderful swimming pool and views across the Cote D'Azure coast. It was a little slice of heaven. It felt so good to be away from the prying eyes and gossip. Margaret Fallows, of course, had been a particular thorn in my side popping in with her false platitudes and enquiries. If I never had to see her again, it would be too soon.

The months we spent there were some of the happiest I've known. Feeling you grow and move inside me was truly wonderful. Some days I'd spend in a shady spot simply stroking my tummy. As the sultry summer days turned to autumn, a seat by the pool became my favourite place. Other days, I'd sit in the kitchen and chat to Mary while she worked. It was a place I was guaranteed to be free from Mother's scrutiny. Once the months turned cooler, I took to the library and read to you from the children's classics or dozed in a comfy chair.

I even had time to think about Robert and what I'd done. I found myself wondering where Francis had put him. Dear Francis, ever the gentleman, would never once have dreamt of burdening the ladies with such gruesome information. I just hoped he'd chosen somewhere secure. The last thing we needed was the body re-appearing. Living with my actions was bad enough without that as well. I'm not heartless, Eve, and I shed many a tear of regret and many a tear of loneliness. My damnable temper and wilful nature had led to this, and as much as I blamed Mother for my inherited behaviours, I couldn't blame her for Robert's death. Accidental or otherwise, the blame for that one lay directly at my door. But as much as I regretted Robert's death, I would always be thankful to him for giving me you.

The rest of the family alternated between clucking over me and insisting on a diet that would have filled an elephant, to anger, and at times, barely contained revulsion. But the 'British Stiff Upper Lip' served us well. The subject of Robert's death was never mentioned, and as the months passed and my body changed, making you more noticeable, the anger and resentment were replaced with a return to something approaching affection. And of course, once you arrived, they were smitten.

You were perfect, from your dark, downy hair to your beautifully shaped fingers and toes. Francis and Helen had agreed to my name choice as long as they could choose your middle name. I'd chosen Eve because it meant 'living' or 'to give life', which seemed somehow apt. Robert had had his life taken, but he had given you yours. As for me, my heart was yours from your first cry. The household felt the same. You healed us in a way nothing else could. You filled us with and wrapped us together with a blanket of love that set everything else to one side. For the first week, nothing marred the magic.

Daddy was the first to burst the bubble. He wanted to send an announcement to the polite world back at home and had come to share his draft notice with us.

'Born in the South of France on 15th March 1947, Eve Victoria. First daughter of Francis and Helen Fenwick. Much loved granddaughter of William and Elizabeth Monmouth. Cherished niece of Doris Monmouth.'

I'd insisted on cherished being added to the notice, but even so, it couldn't alleviate the pain of Helen and Francis claiming you for their own. I felt sick with envy and heartache, but that was Daddy's deal. Helen and Francis would bring you up as theirs. Their names would even appear on the birth certificate. The village gossip at home would simply revel in the delightful news that Helen and Francis's dream had come true. My part of the bargain was to accept the situation and keep quiet. If I did, I could remain at Fremell Hall and watch you grow. I would be a devoted and loving aunt.

What could I do? This was far better than being pushed off to the Welsh Borders to live alone in Robert's house. If I had to be relegated to mere aunt, at least I'd be a well-loved one and on hand in your growing up. Besides, I had a few ideas of my own on that score.

Helen and Francis couldn't have loved you anymore if you had been theirs. You really were a delightful baby. We returned to

Fremell Hall when you were two months old and settled into our new routine. To the outside world, our family and house remained something to look up to. We were the picture of perfect country living, three generations harmoniously sharing our lovely home.

Oddly enough, the reality was pretty harmonious too. Well, for me anyway. Helen and Francis may have been Mummy and Daddy, but I continued to have influence. A lifetime of getting my own way was hard to change. I made my feelings clear about everything from the colour of the nursery to the clothes you wore. Behind closed doors, I was very much the maternal figure. And as Mary remained our only member of permanent staff, there were no curious eyes to see that when little Eve cried, two of us responded. With each cry, Helen and I would meet in the corridor outside your room and do battle for who would attend to you. It was generally me.

Looking back, I can see I didn't make things easy for anyone, especially Helen. I am sorry for that. I know I have been incredibly selfish at times in my life. At least I have the wisdom and grace to acknowledge it.

As you approached your first birthday, Helen and Francis (thankfully without Mother) sat down and told me things had to change. They were going to move out, taking you with them. You deserved a normal home. You needed one mother, not two constantly fighting over you. It made perfect sense. There was no denying it was both the sensible and right thing to do, but inevitably I didn't want to accept it.

I cried and begged. I sobbed and wept. The desolation I felt when Douglas died was nothing compared to this. That had merely broken my heart. This was tearing it to shreds. I promised I'd change. I'd take more of a back seat and let Helen be Mummy. I assured them both I'd focus on being Aunt Doris and nothing more. The crushing reality of how far I'd pushed them sank in. I was terrified that you'd be taken away and I'd be left at Fremell Hall with just Mother and Father. That thought was truly terrifying. Thankfully they seemed to realise I was in earnest, and they agreed to stay another year. Relief flooded through me.

That year was good. We slipped into our newly defined roles, and if I spent hours just gazing at you as you slept, the rest of the slumbering house were none the wiser. You flourished. How could you not when you were surrounded by such love?

Helen and Francis ensured that Wednesday afternoons were just for you and me, and oh how I treasured those days. Doting Aunt Doris could spend it how she liked within the confines of the grounds and village. To be fair to myself, it wouldn't have occurred to me to steal you away. Robert's house (I still didn't regard it as my own) was rented out to tenants and I had no desire to leave Fremell Hall.

One of my favourite places to take you was the Summer House. That probably seems strange given what transpired there but don't forget it was also the place where you were conceived. How could it be anything other than special to me? Plus, it had always been a favourite spot of mine. I couldn't let one small incident change that. I probably sound macabre at best and unhinged at worst, but I truly enjoyed every afternoon spent there. Of course, Mother had done her best to cleanse it of the crime. The rug and chaise longue had been discarded, the comfy chair re-upholstered. Mother had also arranged for new chairs and a table to be brought in. The final touch, a lick of fresh paint had been applied while we were in France awaiting your arrival.

Cocooned in its cosy interior, I sang you nursery rhymes and read my childhood books to you. Inside those wooden walls, your gorgeous chubby fingers explored, touched and discovered. The chairs became your walking aids as you found your feet and started to test your legs. I commissioned a beautiful wooden box to be made that held coloured pencils, paper, toys and games. It lived in the corner and your tottering footsteps took you to it like a homing pigeon. Our little sanctuary was perfect. As you grew steadier on your feet, our Wednesday afternoons started to take in the grounds. We explored the shady wooded paths, searching for fairies, elves and unicorns. Your eyes grew wide with delight when I made up stories about the magical creatures who lived on our land. You were also fascinated by the lake and the ducks. Mary always made sure we had some bread to take with us. There was no such thing as gluten intolerant ducks back then. They got what they were given and were happy.

The first time I lifted you onto my lap on the old tree swing you laughed with delight. Your growing curls tickled my chin as we swung beneath the leafy canopy. I wanted to capture that moment forever. But time doesn't stand still and soon you were hanging onto the swing by yourself. As I pushed you, you called out that you were flying. "I'm flying, Aunty Dodo, like a birdie." You never could say Doris properly and by the time you could, we'd all got used to the nickname.

Despite all our explorations and adventures around the grounds, the stepping stone path to the Summer House remained your favourite and your giggles continued to decorate the walls. The year had slipped by unnoticed into two then approaching three. We'd all relaxed into each other. Even Mother and I became closer. We'd never truly be friends. We were too alike, too wilful and too unwilling to give way to anything other than Helen and Francis's desire for a stable life for you. On that, at least, we were all agreed.

Helen and Francis couldn't do enough for you. You weren't spoilt, though, simply guided through life and encouraged to make the right choices. As much as it pains me to admit it, Helen was a far better mother to you than I would have been. I would have indulged you to the point of ruination. I was a clear example of what getting your own way too often could lead to. Surprisingly, Mother lavished affection on you in a way she never did with her own daughters. This was a side to her Helen and I had never experienced. It made her warmer and softer and far more approachable. I often wonder how different life might have been if she'd treated Helen and I the same way. Father, of course, was once more at the mercies of a small girl child who tugged at his heartstrings, albeit wrapped up in Victorian style constraints.

As for me? I don't have the words to describe how you made me feel. The love seemed to catch in my throat whenever I looked at you. You are probably wondering how on earth I came to leave if this was how I felt. Matters were rather taken out of my hands, darling, and it started with Susan.

I must stop again, Eve, and continue this part of the story another day. I'm exhausted.

Much love
X

CHAPTER 19

At last! A letter that didn't have me recoiling in horror. Instead, emotions of a very different nature warmed me. I could feel the love in every one of Doris's words.

My own personal memories of my childhood married up with what I'd read. I had felt incredibly loved. My grandfather, for all his upright starchy persona, had been deeply attached to Susan and me. We'd wrapped him around our little fingers, and he had doted on us. As for my grandmother, hers was the character I recognised the least from Doris's account so far. With Susan and I, she'd only ever been kind and anything but manipulative. But as grandparents around the world will tell you, we are all much softer and more indulgent with our grandchildren than with their parents. Speaking of parents, Helen and Francis had been wonderful to me. They'd guided mine and Susan's footsteps and nurtured us. Even when they'd broken the news to me about Doris being my mother, they'd done all they could to make it as pain free as possible. I couldn't help but wonder how differently I might have turned out without them. The battles with my temper in my younger days may have developed into something more sinister and damaging if Doris had brought me up. Maybe we'd have clashed as she and Grandmother had. Maybe we'd have been too alike. But that train of thought wasn't one I wished to explore, much less think about.

Although I hadn't lived at Fremell Hall since I was five, I do remember some things. Not specific places, although maybe if I returned there now, I would recognise them. The Summer House, for instance, isn't imprinted on my mind, but maybe it had been in my subconscious when I told Clive I'd like one all those years ago. Shady paths through woodlands have always made me feel secure and safe and I spent hours exploring them with my own children when they were little. To me, they are a leafy cocoon protecting me from the rest of the world outside, no doubt another hangover from my early life. The clearest memory I have is of the tree swing. The feeling of flying through the air while kind hands pushed me feels like yesterday. Funny how I never identified the hands that sent me skyward.

Happy memories and happy words from Doris. It was a relief to read them. The villagers must have looked on with indulgence, approval and maybe some envy too. The Monmouths had weathered the storm of Doris's misfortune with two missing bridegrooms and emerged smiling.

I wished I could remember Doris in person. The photograph she'd enclosed in the first letter had shown me a face that was vaguely familiar or maybe it was just a family resemblance. I needed another look which meant disturbing Clive.

I headed for the door clutching the latest offering from Doris and Benji raised his head, assessed the situation and decided lazing in his bed was the best option. I made my way to the study and waited outside like a nervous patient. I had no idea how Clive would have reacted to Doris's letters. He'd be shocked, no doubt, but would it change our relationship? Would it change how he saw me? I took a breath and tapped gently. I pushed the door open and peered around it. The room was empty. Doris's letters lay strewn across the desk, which was so unlike the meticulous way Clive normally kept paperwork.

My heart lurched, and what-ifs crowded their way in. What if he couldn't face his wife having a murderer for a mother? What if he needed some space away from me? Panic was starting to rise in my chest. Where on earth was he?

Stop it, Eve! For goodness sake, calm down. If he were the one with killer relatives, you'd still love him. The very thought of Clive's staid parents doing anything as illegal as forgetting their road tax, never mind a murder, made me smile. The photo of Doris, Susan and myself was on the far side of the desk. I stretched across and put it in my pocket for perusal later. At this moment, Doris could wait, first I had to find Clive. I left Doris's latest letter with the rest and left the room.

"Clive?" I called up from the bottom of the stairs. "Clive? Are you ok, darling?"

The chain flushed and I heard the taps go on. The bathroom door opened.

"Sorry, Eve, I needed a moment."

Even from the bottom of the stairs and with my less than 20/20 vision, I could see he'd been crying. Cranking my knees into action, I joined him on the landing. He reached out a hand.

"Darling, I'm so sorry. What a shock for you. Come here."

Once more, Clive pulled me close, and we stood entwined. The inevitable floodgates opened and sent forth tears of shock, fear and realisation. I could hear Clive sniffling too. The emotional upheaval of the day washed down my face and onto Clive's shirt. It felt good to release the misery. Without words, we broke our embrace, walked to the bedroom and sat on the edge of our bed.

Neither of us spoke. What could we say? Our lives to date hadn't prepared us for the possibility of this conversation. Eventually, Clive spoke.

"How do you feel about it, Eve?"

"Well, apart from completely flabbergasted and appalled at Doris's actions, I'm not sure, to be honest."

"Any more shocks I should know about?"

"Again, I'm not sure. Doris assures me not, but the

ending of the most recent letter mentioned Susan. I don't even want to think about the implications for that. I can't think rationally about any of this until I finish all the letters."

"Well, let's not think about it then. You keep reading, I'll keep reading and we'll compare notes later. Deal?"

"Deal."

"Now, at risk of you throwing a mug at me, do you want a cup of tea?"

"I didn't think I could face any more of the damned stuff, but actually, that would be lovely. Thanks, love." I leaned over and kissed his cheek before standing up and stretching.

Our knees creaked in unison down the stairs and Benji came to greet us with his wagging stump of a tail. Clive stooped to pat him before carrying on into the kitchen. He filled the kettle and put it on to the Aga. The normality of it all soothed me, and I took Doris's photo out of my pocket. Clive glanced at it.

"You do look like her, you know. Not so much of the Hollywood glamour, but she's definitely left her mark. Her and Helen both."

Clive was right. Whatever Doris had done, she was part of my DNA as indeed was Helen. I just wondered what on earth she still had to reveal. The room at Fremell Hall looked as lovely as Doris, and I had an overwhelming urge to see the place for myself. Maybe once the letters were read and the words sunk in, Clive and I could do some research and go on a little trip. Maybe, but probably not.

In the meantime, my tea was ready and so was I. The next letter awaited.

Letter Number Ten

Dearest Eve,

You had not long turned four when Helen made her announcement. Like last time, she gripped my hands when she told me she was pregnant. A bloom of joy and hope coloured her cheeks and she'd never looked more beautiful. She was clearly over the moon.

Unlike last time, she'd waited to tell me. She'd even waited before telling Francis. She wanted to be past the stage of the pregnancy when she'd lost the last baby before telling anyone. With Francis in the know, the rest of us received her news with delight. At four months pregnant, she was feeling better than she had during the previous time and she was ready to shout it from the rooftops.

Of course, Fremell Hall was thrown into a flurry of excitement, and we also launched into full-on 'Protect Helen' mode. Mother insisted Dr Caldbeck come to visit every week. Once he'd seen Helen, Mother would quiz him over tea and cake before he was allowed to leave. Everything but everything he suggested must be followed to the letter. Helen would be the best patient he'd ever had. Mother would see to it all.

Mary was instructed to cook whatever Helen desired. She was also instructed to cook some of the less palatable things Dr Caldbeck had suggested as well. Helen forced it down and thought of the baby. We employed a day girl from the village who was tasked with a thorough clean of the nursery and to relieve some of Mary's duties so she could devote herself to catering for Helen. One of the local men was given the job of applying a new coat of paint to the nursery. Francis made it his mission to keep Helen happy and stress-free and I was ordered on no account to upset her in any way.

It was almost as if Mother read my mind.

I was genuinely delighted when Helen told me. I wanted her to experience pregnancy and feel her child grow. She was my sister and I loved her. She truly deserved happiness. I can't lie, though, Eve. Once the immediate glow had faded, I began to think about the coming baby as a beacon of hope. Could there be the chance that Helen would become so wrapped up in the new child that she'd be happy for you to spend more time with me? The idea thrilled me. Visions of becoming Mummy in all but name chased through my mind. Mother's protective shield only added to this.

"You shouldn't be carrying Eve up to bed now. She's getting too big." Mother's voice was sharp and anxious.

So, of course, I was only too happy to step in and oblige. Your little arms clung around my neck and the tip of your nose nudged my cheek as you wrapped your legs around my waist. Each stair was like a step towards paradise. For that glorious minute every day, you were mine. Sometimes your head drooped on my shoulder, and sometimes we sang our way up. Letting you go at the top was always a wrench, but bedtime story was still Helen's domain and one she was not willing to relinquish. I couldn't blame her.

Mother's infernal knitting needles set to work once more. With each knit one purl one, she handed out more orders to the rest of the house. How Francis was able to stand it, I don't know. His own large family home though busy and chaotic with siblings must surely have seemed a better option sometimes. A quiet, dignified man he may have been, but he wasn't a pushover and living under your grandmother's rule must have irritated him beyond measure. He'd obviously weighed up the cost of living with Mother versus living in and one day being master of Fremell Hall and decided it all balanced out.

The only person who didn't seem as enthusiastic as I would have expected was Daddy. Oh, he made the right noises. He'd kissed Helen's cheek, patted Francis on the back and raised glasses in a toast, but I could sense something was wrong. I found him in the library one day staring at the pages of a book. He looked utterly alone and haggard. Useless to ask him, of course. Daddy was very much of the era when men categorically did not talk about their feelings. Maybe if I'd spoken out... Maybe is a big word.

The rest of Helen's pregnancy passed by. You were, in turn, curious and utterly unimpressed by the thought of a new sibling. I bought you a doll with little cloth nappies and clothes, and we played babies. Whether it helped to prepare you or not, you enjoyed the game. When you put the 'baby' on the tree swing and swung it high using the same words I used when I pushed you, my heart skipped a beat. A sibling would be good for you. The company of other children was the only thing you truly lacked. We had avoided the thought of school so far, but that would have to be addressed soon. In the meantime, a brother or sister would help fill the gap.

When your sister Susan decided it was time to make her appearance, we'd just shown the vicar off following elevenses. Mother was organising an event at the Village Hall, and any last-minute details could always be ironed out over a plate of Mary's scones. Thankfully, Daddy was in his study with his man of business, Jordan, because Helen's waters broke all over the hearthrug. Daddy would have been mortified to face this most natural of human conditions. As luck would have it, Francis had just got back from running an errand, and between them, he and Mother got Helen up the stairs and into her bedroom.

With strict instructions to ring Dr Caldbeck and keep you occupied, I was soon from everyone's mind. Leaving Mary to await the doctor's arrival, you and I retreated to our favourite spot in the Summer House. As ever, you jumped along the stepping stones spaced throughout the grass. Your curls bounced with each leap and I reflected on how much simpler life is when you are four. Life probably seems anything but simple at the moment for you, Eve, and I do apologise for disrupting your world with my letters.

During the afternoon, I tried to imagine what it would be like with another baby in the house. It would certainly change the dynamic again. This time I would be an aunty in every sense of the word.

Susan Frances Fenwick made her appearance with minimal fuss on October 17th. Helen bore her pains stoically as I would have expected. Once Mother had deemed her fit to receive visitors, Francis was ushered in to meet his daughter. Although I'd expected to lead you in to meet Susan, it was Francis who held your hand lovingly and took you to peer at a wrinkled red face. I edged into the room and was brought up by the vision in front of me.

The four of you made a beautiful picture. Helen was as serene and calm as an angel bestowing love from every pore onto the child in her arms. Francis looked on proudly as you scrambled up to see the baby. Looking at you all, I knew my hopes that Helen would be engrossed in the new child and leave you to me were futile. Helen pulled you in closer and wrapped a protective arm around you while holding Susan in the other. The Fenwick Family Unit was complete, and I was neither needed nor required.

I closed the door softly and left.

Over the next few weeks, Mother was euphoric once she'd got over her initial disappointment that Susan was yet another girl. The congratulations and visits from the villagers had been denied to her when you were born. She intended to revel in every minute of her success this time. Chief among the visitors was my old nemesis Margaret Fallows of course. She cooed over Susan, announced that she and Mr Fellows were expecting a second of their own and had the nerve to ask if I had ever heard anything from Robert or if I was hoping to find fiancé number three. She knew a lovely eligible man who would be just perfect. There was no way she could resist gloating over what she saw as my spinsterish, barren existence. If only she knew...

If only I'd known that Margaret Fallows was going to prove a thorn in the side not only for me but also for the whole Monmouth family, I think I would have killed her right there and then. And Mother would probably have helped me.

I am getting ahead of myself, and once again, my body is telling me to rest, Eve. I must listen to it in a way I never did in my youth. We take our physical wellness for granted. It's hard to accept that there are limitations you no longer have any control over. Ageing is something I resent, but it is the only thing certain in life other than taxes. Ah yes, taxes, but that my dear must wait for the next letter.

Much love
X

CHAPTER 21

It was a relief to read that Susan had had a normal, straightforward, uncomplicated conception and birth. I don't think I could have coped with anything more dramatic. Casting my mind back, I couldn't remember the day Susan was born, but I do remember the baby doll. It was the same dolly we'd had tea with on the day Doris left. I pulled the photograph out of my pocket and there she was on the chair next to me. The same dolly my children and grandchildren had played with. Only now, with the great-grandchild, had Dolly finally been allowed some rest. She was becoming too fragile after three generations of loving but less than gentle hands.

The tea set hadn't survived. Back then, it was considered perfectly acceptable to give real china tea sets to children. It's a miracle any of them made it through the first tea party! And now, thanks to my lamentable temper, mine and Clive's tea service was ruined too. I bit my lip. I'd tried so hard over the years to keep the need to lash out in check.

For most of my adult life, I've been remarkably calm, but I'd battled with anger as a teenager. It made perfect sense now why my parents had watched me warily during these outbursts. They were obviously terrified I'd inherited Doris's, and so it would appear, my grandmother's short fuse. They'd quickly arranged for me to see a doctor about my nerves. Why did they never call it what it was? Nerves is such a wishy-washy term. I spoke to nurses, doctors and psychotherapists and eventually found my way through.

By the time I met Clive, I was content to live on a plateau of tranquillity. I'm not denying there have been times in my life when that plateau has been somewhat shaky. But all in all, the techniques I learnt have stood me well. Until now...

I'd have to look into getting the teapot repaired. Maybe that Japanese technique of repairing it without masking the break would be best. It would be a stark reminder about the fragility of human emotion. I pulled myself out of the chair and made my way to the front room. My phone was charging up. Our children were always telling us there was no point in having a mobile phone if we didn't keep it with us! I detached it from the USB point and shivered. It was cold in here after the warmth of the sunroom. I didn't hang around. Once I was settled in my chair again, I activated my phone screen and typed in 'Japanese pottery repair gold', and the power of the internet amazed me once more. From that vague and disjointed phrase, exactly what I was looking for appeared before my eyes.

'Kintsugi (golden joinery) or Kintsukuroi (golden repair) is the Japanese art of repairing pottery. Breakages are mended with lacquer which is dusted or mixed with powdered silver, gold or platinum. Both the breakage and repair are part of the history of the object and not something that needs disguising. The philosophy is all about embracing the flawed and imperfect.'

Flawed and imperfect. Well, that certainly summed up humanity pretty well. And it most definitely summed up Doris and her revelations. My life story as I knew it had been shattered and broken into many pieces. Instead of trying to ignore or pretend it hadn't happened, I needed to embrace it. I had to accept it as part of the new me. My life would be repaired and Clive would be the gold to keep me together. Having a mother as a killer was alarming and terrifying and completely unbelievable, but the cracks this knowledge had caused could be made good again, I was sure. Already I knew that I'd have to allow myself to process all the information Doris had flung at me today. My own fragility needed some essential repair work too.

And in the meantime, I still had to decide what to do about Susan. My history affected her history. We'd always confided in each other. The thought of keeping something like this from her just wasn't something I could contemplate. I picked up my phone again. There was a missed call from her. She must have tried this number before the landline earlier. My thumb hovered over the redial button. Like Pandora, once I let this out, there would be no putting it back. Susan would be embroiled in it all as much as I. Did I really want to put her through that? But would she forgive me if I didn't? Ring or not ring?

As the ringtone erupted and made me jump, the decision it seemed was being taken out of my hands. It was Susan.

"Are you ok, Eve? Not like you to shower in the middle of the day."

"I'm fine, Sue. I'd been gardening and worked up a bit of a sweat. I was just about to ring you, as it happens. Do you want to come around tomorrow? I've had some rather interesting post I need to tell you about."

"And now you want me to wait until tomorrow! You can't drop a carrot like that into the conversation and then expect me to wait." Susan was rightly indignant.

"I know! I'm sorry, but I haven't got to the bottom of it myself yet. There are still a few letters to go. Come for lunch. I'll tell you everything then, I promise. Look, I'll have to go, or I won't have them finished before I see you."

"Very well, but this better be worth it and not some boring old letter from a long lost relative we have no desire to meet."

"Ha, you are so right and so wrong at the same time. See you tomorrow." I ended the call amid Susan's spluttered response.

I knew I hadn't been fair to her. Her curiosity would be eating her up. Half a story can be so frustrating, but that was all I had for now. The remaining pile of unread letters was pretty small, so the final pieces couldn't be far off. I took a deep breath and prepared myself for Doris's next instalment.

Letter Number Eleven

Darling Eve,

Susan's arrival wasn't the only thing to change the dynamic of Fremell Hall that year.

Taxes—the scourge of the rich and poor alike. The previous five years had seen death duties raised not once, not twice, but three times. Obviously, Daddy would normally have kept such mundane information from his girls. We were to be kept out of business and not be worried about money, and we had done our best to follow this. Following the first war and prior to the second coming along with its privations and losses for all, Mother had insisted upon the best of everything.

The second war curbed her spending to a degree and, of course, a decimated workforce coupled with a countrywide tightening of the belt had meant we no longer had staff for every whim and task. This was something we'd all been extremely grateful for when Robert died. But, with the war well and truly over, Mother seemed keen to spend again. She had plans, big plans, and they were going to start with the garden.

The latest rise in death duties came into play during 1949 and, coupled with the two previous rises in 1945 and 1947, were to have a catastrophic impact upon the Monmouths. Poor Daddy. While we delighted in your arrival and then Susan's, he was busy trying to keep the roof over our heads.

The levies imposed on properties ranging from small country manors to stately homes would prove the downfall of many a family residence. Daddy knew that remaining in the hall would be unsustainable. He also knew that with his passing, all we'd inherit was a beautiful house we couldn't afford to live in. By the time

Susan was born, he was already looking for buyers. He just hadn't told Mother yet!

Daddy was a rigid, upright man and the thought of discussing such an issue with his wife was utterly abhorrent to him. This was the way of the world back then. Mother may have been a strong, formidable character, but their marriage was still very much a product of the time. Eventually, though, he'd had no choice. Daddy informed us over breakfast that he'd be meeting with Jordan, and it was vital they were not to be disturbed. He promised to explain it all once the meeting was over, but we must prepare ourselves for some news. It didn't sound good. Even worse, when Jordan arrived, instead of greeting us warmly like he usually did, he gave a brief nod to Mother before following Daddy into the study with a grim face. They remained there for the morning and didn't even ring for Mary to bring tea.

Mother was like a cat on hot bricks. The little jacket she was making for Susan lay untouched on her lap. The lack of clicking needles only added to the tension which filled the room and infected us all. When Mary came to announce lunch, it was a relief to have something to do. You, of course, had remained oblivious. Dolly and Teddy had occupied both your mind and hands.

Mother was pushing her food around her plate when Daddy finally came in and joined us. Jordan had left without taking formal leave of us. This was also most unusual as he usually joined us for lunch after a morning of business. Daddy looked so alone when he entered the dining room. He was grey-faced and wandered aimlessly to the sideboard to fill his plate with things he wouldn't eat. He seemed beyond our reach and somehow, we all felt this was a pivotal moment in our family. Even my transgressions hadn't made him look so bleak and lost.

Daddy sat at the table staring at his plate until eventually he simply asked Mother if she'd join him for a walk in the garden. This was an activity so unlike him. I was instantly filled with dread. If this morning's visitor had been Dr Caldbeck instead of Jordan, I would have been certain he'd received a death sentence. He and Mother disappeared out onto the terrace, down the steps and turned left to begin their perambulations. As soon as they were out of sight, the atmosphere changed.

You still needed to be encouraged to finish your lunch and Francis was encouraging Helen to eat something before Susan awoke and needed feeding. Mary bustled in, removing dishes from the sideboard in her usual manner. Normality returned for a little while, but it wasn't to last.

When they returned, Daddy and Mother both looked terrible. Mother was drained of colour and looked positively ghastly. Daddy summoned Mary and asked her to take you to the kitchen to make scones. You scampered off in ignorant bliss, no doubt excited at the prospect of counting sultanas and helping with the mixture. How I wished I too could bury myself in Mary's warm and comforting kitchen as Helen and I had done as children. As soon as you left the room, Daddy sat down heavily in his chair. He didn't seem to know where to start. Mother wasn't looking at him. It was almost as if she couldn't bear to. When the news came, it was totally unexpected and a complete blow.

Fremell Hall, while not a huge mansion, was a comfortable Georgian house. It had eight bedrooms, attic rooms for servants, a drawing room, living room, dining room, library, study, conservatory and generous kitchen and pantry. Outside, a coach house and stable block were inevitably full of cars and old bits of antiquated gardening equipment. One hundred acres of land, including a small wood, lake and access to the quarry where the stone which built the house came from, completed its attractions. All told, it was an elegant residence and there had been Monmouths there for several generations. None of them had been particularly remarkable or noteworthy. It was simply a nice house for a nice family. But nice, elegant houses require money and Daddy's funds were running low. The only feasible option was to sell while he still could.

So that was why Daddy looked so grim-faced and Mother so utterly heartbroken. Our beautiful home would have to be sold. Helen and Francis would no longer inherit, and neither would you. Your birth right was gone. You would not grow up knowing and loving each brick as I had. Unbelievably, worse was still to come. Daddy already had a buyer...John Fallows.

That's right, Margaret Fallows, my old nemesis, her husband and their children would be living in our house! The humiliation was too much to bear. Margaret Fallows rubbing our noses in it, lording it up around our home. And what of us? Where would we go? Where would we live? Now clearly wasn't the time to ask Daddy. He looked like a shell of the man I'd known all my life. Francis poured him a brandy and placed the glass in his hand. With shaking hands, Daddy drank, and thankfully the greyness left his face.

The thought of leaving Francis and Helen a lifetime of debt was unforgivable as far as he was concerned. The only solution was to sell and downsize. Robert's house, which I still struggled to think of as mine, was a comfortable five-bedroom house, but even with a generous price ticket, it wouldn't be enough to cover the cost of Fremell Hall. I offered it, of course. Daddy thanked me sweetly but shook his head. I don't know what upset him more, the thought of his daughter having to bail him out or the thought of effectively making us all homeless.

I'd been so determined for my children to be born at Fremell Hall that it had led to Robert's death. What a crushing realisation to face. None of my future children would now be born or indeed live there. It pierced me to my heart. Anger, remorse and disbelief were on a relay around my bloodstream. The needless death of a good man weighed me down more at that moment than any other.

We all sat like stones, unmoving and unable to speak. What on earth would the future hold for us all, and how would it affect you? Where would Francis and Helen live? And what would it mean for me? At this point, I knew I'd have to come up with some kind of plan, however drastic that may be.

I'm sorry, Eve. my heart is pounding and my head aches. The staff here hover around me at various points during the day. They don't approve of my exerting myself so much. They think I should be content to wait for death in a quiet and calm manner, but that's never been my style.

I'll keep writing until the story is told, and then my love, it's up to you. You will be the curator and it will be for you to decide what to do with it. We're near the end now, I promise.

All my love
X

CHAPTER 23

My stomach flipped a little at the final sentence in the letter. Doris was clearly a lady with limited time left for her. She was obviously in some kind of establishment that provided care and that was reassuring. This woman who, until this morning, had barely featured in my life or thoughts over the years had somehow got right under my skin and into my heart. Despite her actions, I felt sad at the thought of her dying. Yes, she'd presented me with some shocking truths, but she had also provided me with links and an insight into my family. How strange to feel so emotional about a woman I hadn't seen for nearly seventy years.

I hadn't even thought about the possibility of meeting her in person until now. Reading about her weakened state revealed how old and vulnerable she really was. I rapidly did the calculations in my head. Unless I was way off, Doris must be ninety-two. A good age even by today's standards. Was she even still alive at this point? For all I knew, she could have instructed these letters to be delivered after her death. If she was still alive, what on earth would we talk about? And did I want to try and see her anyway? I didn't have the answers to those questions yet.

My thoughts returned to the last part of the letter and the decision that would be mine to make regarding her story. Was she expecting me to report this? Confess her sins for her? Please don't let her task me with finding Robert's body. The previous Monmouths may have been unremarkable and nothing of note, but Doris certainly wasn't. Nothing would surprise me now.

What did surprise me was how suddenly hungry I felt. Whether it was Doris's reassurance that her story was nearly complete or my body refusing to take anything else without food, I needed to eat. There was a good homemade broth in the fridge. I'd warm some through with a bread bun. Comfort food was definitely required, and Clive could probably do with some too. As if reading my mind, Benji padded from the sunroom into the kitchen and up the corridor towards Clive's study.

I busied myself with the broth, pan, Aga and bowls. I sliced the buns, buttered them and laid them on plates either side of the soup bowls. Then I turned my attention to the soup itself; it was Mary's old recipe. Simply stirring it was very soothing. Fragments of Doris's letters floated through my mind like the carrots and barley in the broth. Shame they weren't quite so tasty and wholesome! The question of what to do with Doris's story was one I couldn't answer until I had the whole tale. Thoughts were vying for space in my mind when Clive appeared.

"Hello love, how are you bearing up? Any more shocks?"

"Nothing too horrendous since the earlier letters. How are you getting on with my sordid family secrets?"

"Well, it's a lot to take in. I'm glad of a break. I didn't realise how hungry I was until I smelt your broth."

I smiled. I often joked that I won Clive's heart with potatoes, carrots and barley. Giving the spoon a final turn, I lifted the pan off the heat and shared it between our bowls—another relic from our wedding day.

"I've spoken to Susan. She rang back when the phone was in my hand."

"And...?"

"She's coming tomorrow for lunch. I said I'd fill her in then. I'm not sure whether to tell her or give her the letters to read for herself. What do you think?"

"The letters bring it to life vividly, that's for sure, and I definitely think it will be easier than trying to explain it. I think you'd lose your thread. There's so much to remember. Plus, it might upset you if you have to verbalise it all, and you might not get the words out for tears." Clive was ever the voice of reason.

"Yes, I think you're right. I hope we have enough broth left for tomorrow's lunch. I'm not sure I have the energy to rustle anything else up."

"I can make sandwiches if need be; don't worry. Susan will have other things to think of once she gets reading anyway."

"True enough! I'm dreading it if I'm honest. What on earth will she think, Clive?"

"That she has a wonderful sister who makes wonderful broth. Doris's letters won't change that."

I patted Clive's hand. Ever calm, ever practical. Marriage to a GP had had its fair share of stresses and worries over the years, but his bedside manner had always been excellent—even for family.

"I've decided to have the teapot mended with that Japanese gold technique. You know, they enhance the repair rather than hide it. That seems apt somehow."

"Are you sure you wouldn't rather just get rid of it?" Clive looked concerned.

"No. It represents our marriage and our love. The fact that I broke it because of my temper is no reason to discard it. It would be like throwing away our memories. I know that sounds daft because we've hardly used it over the last few years, but it's part of us. I won't let Doris impact that. It will also be a reminder that things can be repaired and carry on. It seems, oh I don't know, somehow symbolic of me."

Clive nodded and spooned more broth into his mouth. He seemed reassured by my response. The calm and reasonable Eve was in control.

"Will you stack the bowls in the dishwasher? I want to get these letters finished. There's only a couple left now."

"Of course, and don't worry, it will all work out."

I leant across the table and kissed his brow before standing up. Benji had obviously had enough of my company staying by Clive's feet under the table as I returned to the sunroom. For what felt like the hundredth time, I picked up the top envelope, tore it open and began to read.

Letter Number Twelve

Dearest Eve,

We moved around the Hall in shock for the next couple of days. Mother barely spoke. Helen alternated from crying to over-the-top cheerfulness, which was more draining than her tears. I, on the other hand, was angry. Daddy assured us we could have one more Christmas here, but the Fallows wanted to take possession by April at the latest. This meant we'd be leaving not long after your fifth birthday. When I think of what I went through to keep you in this house, a cauldron of rage burned deep within me. I'd killed Robert, however accidental that had been because I wanted you to enjoy the woods, the lake, the Summer House and the life that went with Fremell Hall. I had knocked the life out of a good, decent man for an objective that was now utterly futile.

I wanted to scream and shout—most of all, I wanted to break and smash things. And one morning, I did exactly that. As I stood in the living room with its lovely fireplace and tasteful furniture, the thought of Margaret's vulgar touch made bile rise in my throat. Before I knew it, one of the uglier vases on the mantelpiece was in pieces on the floor. Mother entered hurriedly to find me with angry tears starting from my eyes. Taking in the scene with a cool glance, she crunched her way through the pieces, picked up the remaining matching vase and sent that crashing to the floor.

We looked at each other, and in that moment, we were bonded like never before. I reached out a shaking hand, uncertain of how it would be received. Mother clung to it and pulled me into a crushing hug. Our emotions broke, noisily at first, but eventually, the heaving sobs passed, and shaky breaths and undignified snuffles took over. Some instinct caused us both to step back at the same time. Mother approached the mirror, which looked strangely different without the vases in front of it. She patted her hair, dabbed her

*cheeks with a handkerchief and left the room. We never spoke of it
again, but relations were somewhat warmer between us for a while.*

*While we were smashing chinaware, Daddy and Francis
were yet again hidden away in the study. They were discussing
'family options', as they called it. Daddy had been made to promise
to keep nothing else from us and he kept to his word giving us a
little progress report each evening before dinner. This was now the
third day they'd been talking over ideas. I decided it was time to add
my own suggestion to the mix. Like Mother, I patted my hair,
dabbed my cheeks and made my way to the study. I needed to
convince them that my idea would work.*

*I had a perfectly good house. Admittedly, I'd never seen it,
had never until now had any desire to, but it was there. It would be
a squeeze for us all and I wasn't even sure if there would be
accommodation for Mary. But at least we'd all be together. I thought
it would be a good solution, but their response was not what I
expected.*

*Francis wanted to move to the Scottish Borders. He had
an old aunt up there who had always doted on him. She sent the
most divine shortbread at regular intervals and he and Helen
normally spent at least one weekend a year visiting Aunt Annabel.
She'd already told Francis he was named in her will. There
wouldn't be any property, but there was a substantial amount of
money. Certainly enough to buy a modest but nice house and give
them a fresh start. Francis had already been making enquiries
about transferring his Civil Service job to Edinburgh. It all sounded
settled with very little fuss.*

*I have to be honest, I'd never really thought about Scotland
before. It had always seemed so far away and Helen had complained
about the midges and the cold. Needs must, though, and we'd all*

have to cut our cloth. We'd just need to make sure it was weatherproof. We could all adjust, and as long as we were all together, that was the main thing.

It seems that was not the main thing at all. Francis felt it was time for Helen and the girls to have a home just for themselves. He was terribly sorry, but I wouldn't be moving in with them. At first, I thought he must be addressing Daddy and I could understand him wanting to be away from my mother's forceful personality. The realisation that he was actually talking to me was crushing. Francis and Helen's future plans did not include me at all. Daddy and Mother were going to buy somewhere with the proceeds left over from the sale of Fremell Hall after settling the outstanding debts. I would have to live with them like some unwanted maiden aunt. I was now surplus to requirement.

No longer would I see you first thing with your hair matted and your cheeks flushed from sleep. Your giggle wouldn't echo around my home. You wouldn't climb into my bed on Sunday mornings for a story. Our special little bond would be stretched and stretched until inevitably you became wholly Helen's.

They didn't even want to talk about Robert's house. The decision was made. The Scottish Borders were calling, and the Monmouths and Fenwicks would be setting up new establishments there. In one fell swoop, I was to lose you and the Hall. I couldn't bear to think of it.

A sort of madness came over me. Looking back from the here and now, I can see that my emotional state had been brittle since Douglas's death. Robert's demise at my hands had weakened it further. This was the final straw. Something in me cracked.

I put on a very good show of convincing everyone (myself included) that I was fine. I immersed myself in the preparations for Christmas. If this were to be our last as a family under one roof, it would be truly magnificent. Mother and I were on the same page for this. It was a strange and tense time. Outsiders would have seen our preparations and been envious of the idyllic Christmas scene we were creating. Inside, it was fraying at every corner and the loose threads were tangling us all.

Mother insisted on the biggest tree we'd ever had. It was enormous and took days to install and decorate. Poor Mary was baking cinnamon twists and gingerbread men for what felt like weeks. You helped her, and your stodgy sweet offerings were hung with pride from the fragrant branches. Like every year, we turned our Summer House into a grotto for the local children to come and meet Father Christmas. You were at that magical age when he was a reality rather than a nostalgic memory. Without you, we'd have descended into a mass of self-pity and woe. You kept us focused on the spirit of the festive season. Mother organised a cocktail party and a wreath making morning. They were hugely successful. Visitors gasped at the tree and when you appeared in a red dress trimmed with white, everyone said you were the most beautiful Christmas decoration in the house. The only thing to mar it was Margaret Fallows with her tasteless and loudly declared plans for changes at the Hall. Christmas at Fremell Hall would be very different next year, she told anyone who'd listen. Mother and I exchanged glances. God, we hated her.

The Christmas Dance had to be attended as well. The village would expect a final swansong from the Monmouths. None of us were enthusiastic but felt compelled by obligation. I have no recollection of what I wore for that event, although I do remember it was a beautiful frosty, crisp night. As usual, we walked there, but unlike other occasions, we were silent. A deep melancholy washed over me when we arrived at the familiar building. The bunting and decorations were the same as they'd always been. It seemed so solid, so unchanging, so immovable, so like the Monmouths used to be. We fixed on our smiles and showed our public faces to the world. I couldn't help but recall dances from other occasions. This time, the ghosts of Douglas and Robert swirled around the room with me. Their faces blurred, merged, and at times, seemed to mock me. I'd never been so glad to leave. For once, I left early with Daddy and Mother.

It took us half an hour to get away. It seemed the world and his wife wanted to tell us how sorry they were we were leaving. Daddy handled it all with his usual stiff upper lip and Mother gritted her teeth and smiled politely. I don't remember what I said, something nondescript and perfectly acceptable, I hope.

The final days leading up to Christmas dragged. Now there was no changing it, and I wanted it done. I wanted to leave and get away. Our new life was waiting to begin, and I was becoming impatient and feverish with anticipation. My heart jumbled and bumped along while my nerves were shot to pieces. Loud noises made me flinch and I was desperately trying to put the finishing touches to my plan.

The days between Christmas and New Year are always such a drag. A listlessness takes over and the anticipation of the New Year and what it will bring is a carrot dangling on a stick that seems to go on forever. This year was very different, and I had things to pack and organise. I had to make sure I had everything we'd need. 1952 would be a year like no other. New Year's Eve itself passed without our usual cocktail party. None of us had the appetite for it. Instead, we spent an idyllic early evening playing games with you. You giggled delightedly and helped us to forget our troubles for a while. When Helen carried you upstairs, you took the joy and laughter with you and we were left sitting deflated and unmoving.

Mary arrived with a tray of tea and tidied up the games we'd enjoyed so enthusiastically before you went to bed. She had accepted the move with far more stoicism than we had. Mary would oversee a thorough cleaning and itemising of the house contents. Nobody knew better what we actually had. She had lovingly cleaned and polished it all for most of her life. And it was she who would choose the kitchen utensils which would be accompanying the family to Scotland. Mother had come to rely upon her even more than usual. I would miss her terribly, but it was time for me to forge a new path. From now on, you would be all the family I needed.

The New Year crept into the room, and we didn't even bother with the usual tradition of taking the old year out through the back and bringing the new one in through the front. It all seemed rather pointless. I couldn't recall a New Year when the occupants of Fremell Hall had been in bed before the early hours.

I have no recollection of New Year's Day itself. No doubt Mary will have fed us lavishly, roast beef probably. Inevitably she'd have made her special New Year cake which I have tried and failed to replicate over the years. Even after all this time, I can imagine the taste of it. But I digress.

Wednesday 2nd January 1952 was to be the start of our new life together. I'd barely slept the night before and my heart was pounding. My head ached, but I pushed that aside in order to focus on the day. Nobody thought it strange when we walked out of the door hand in hand. It was Wednesday, after all; it was our day together. The only difference was our destination wasn't the Summer House. This time I told you we were going on a big adventure in a car, just the two of us.

I battled to keep my emotions in check as I turned to look at the place that had been my home. A place that, despite everything, was largely full of happy, content, idyllic memories. A house I had presumed would be yours one day. My hands shook as I helped you into the car. I'd loaded the boot up the night before. We were free to go. Yet still, I was kept rooted to the ground— Monmouth ground. It felt comfortable and right beneath my feet. Leaving was such a wrench, but it was time to go.

You asked me where we were going and I simply replied, "Wherever we want to, darling."

The tyres moved over the gravel with a satisfying crunch. My hands gripped the steering wheel tightly as we proceeded down the driveway. I had no clear plan of where we were going. I hadn't even thought where we would stay that night. I didn't care. The two of us would make our own path from now on.

As the driveway joined the road, I halted and looked each way undecided. "Which way, darling?" I asked you. And you pointed left. Left it was.

My head was aching quite abominably by now and my breathing was more than a little ragged. Excitement and nervous energy coursed through my veins. We were free! I wouldn't have to share you with anyone from now on. I would be your mummy. I would be the one to put you to bed, brush your beautiful hair and tell you stories every night. Aunty Dodo would be no more. Rationality had long deserted me.

I remember feeling incredibly elated but also insufferably hot. My cheeks were flying two spots of colour when I glanced in the rear-view mirror. I was finding it hard to concentrate or to decide where to drive. My heart felt as if it would leap out of my chest onto the bonnet. I shook my head in an attempt to focus. I glanced at you, and you smiled. That smile was worth everything.

To this day, I have no recollection of the crash. Apparently, I veered onto the wrong side of the road and we hit a telephone box. When help came, I was unconscious over the steering wheel and you were crying for Helen. I've often wondered what might have happened if you'd told me to go right instead.

When I came round, I was in a hospital bed and Mother was by my side. My thoughts turned immediately to you. Where were you? Were you all right? Beyond assuring me that you were unharmed, Mother said very little else. She just sat there with her infernal knitting. The needles clackety clacked until the inside of my brain was screaming. I was screaming! Nurses flooded the room, a needle jabbed my arm and the blessed darkness deafened the knitting for a while.

I don't remember much about my stay in hospital, but after a week, I was deemed well enough to return to civilisation. Civilisation just wasn't ready for me.

The next part of my life is painful to write, and I can't quite face it today. Tomorrow my darling, I will draw this sorry tale to a conclusion, I promise.

All my love
X

CHAPTER 25

Just when I thought Doris couldn't shock me anymore, she went ahead and did it anyway. Not content with murder (albeit accidental), now it appeared she was guilty of kidnap. What on earth must Helen and Francis have felt when they realised I was missing? I couldn't imagine the horror that must have passed through them. I remember losing sight of Marianne in a shop once and the thump of my heart had almost broken my rib cage. It had been the longest five minutes of my life. Helen and Francis must have been frantic. Not only did they have to come to terms that I'd been taken but also with the fact that the culprit was Helen's own sister.

Like Doris, I couldn't help but wonder how different my life could have been if we'd turned right. Would we have driven off into the sunset with a golden future to look forward to? Probably not. If Doris's mental and physical well-being were so compromised and fragile, the outcome would probably have been the same. I was lucky we hadn't been badly injured. I screwed my eyes up and cast my mind back, but no memories stirred. I had no recollection of the accident at all, which is probably a good thing. It must have been very frightening for my younger self to be alone in a car with an unconscious woman.

Even allowing for a mother's love and her delicate state, there was no denying Doris had crossed a whole new line. As much as I loved Susan, if she'd attempted to snatch either of my children and then involved them in an accident, I'd struggle to maintain a relationship with her. I can only presume this was the final straw and the catalyst for Doris's departure.

Just two envelopes remained now. The final one was very thin. At a guess, I'd say it held a single sheet of paper. The other envelope was considerably more substantial. It seemed strange to think that it held the final part of the story. I had a feeling it also held confusion and yet more questions. I wasn't hopeful that the contents would bring me either answers or closure.

I drained the remaining water in my glass and nipped into the kitchen to refill it. A trip to the bathroom was much needed as well. As I headed up the corridor, Clive and Benji were nowhere to be seen. No doubt they were in the study. Benji would have ensconced himself on Clive's knee as usual.

To save my creaking knees, I used the small toilet under the stairs that we'd had fitted some years previously. I let the water wash over my wrists and I splashed my face to freshen up.

My head was a little achy, probably dehydration. Clive was always telling me to drink more. Back in the kitchen, I filled my glass again, but I wasn't quite ready to re-enter Doris's world. I wasn't hungry, but I opened the fridge anyway. Nothing tempted me. The biscuit tin, however, did. At seventy-two, it was a little late to discover comfort eating, but I couldn't help it.

The digestive crunched satisfyingly. I fished another one out of the tin and returned to my chair in the sunroom. The sun had moved around further and its rays now shone over the back of the Summer House. It seemed to highlight the building and my eyes were pulled towards it. I shuddered again. I'd have to do something to rid myself of that horror. I couldn't let my sanctuary become sullied and tarnished by events that hadn't even taken place there.

I stood up and drew the curtain partway across the window until the Summer House was hidden from view. That decisive action seemed to spur me on. I took my place once more and reached for the end of the story.

Letter Number Thirteen

Darling Eve,

The doctors had said I could return home where I would need calm and quiet. I was ecstatic. The thought of being reunited with you had sustained me during this dark time. I couldn't wait to hold you in my arms. Understandably relations would probably be a little strained between us all, but I was looking forward to rejoining the family. I fully expected my room to be waiting, freshly aired with nice crisp sheets. No doubt Helen would have picked some snowdrops to scent the room and lift my mood.

Reality, however, did not live up to my expectation. From underneath the blanket Mother had wrapped around me, I started to notice the landscape outside the car window. We were not heading in the direction of the Hall.

"Where are we going?" I'd asked in some alarm. As much as I was apprehensive about the initial meeting with Helen and Francis, the thought of seeing you again was enough for me to be impatient.

"It's for the best, Doris. You need quiet and you need calm. You heard the doctors." Mother's voice was like ice.

"How can I be calm if I can't see Eve? She's my daughter!"

"No, she's not Doris. She's Helen's. It was Helen she called for when you crashed. It was Helen she clung to in terror when we got her back to the house. It was Helen, not you, who made her feel safe again."

Each word cut my soul. The one person in the world I would willingly die for and I had terrified you. I'd made you scared

154

and vulnerable. I was no mother figure. I was no mother. The rest of the journey passed in bleak despair. I barely noticed when Daddy turned off the road and drove up the gravelled driveway to a genteel looking house.

I was welcomed warmly to The Towers. Matron was kindly but not one to brook any kind of nonsense from anyone. I overheard her and my parents discussing me.

"Nerves."

"Total rest, not to be alarmed."

"No visitors apart from us." This was Daddy. He'd never sounded so cold. Even he had turned his back on me.

Mother brushed my cheek with cold lips. Daddy patted my hand and, at the last moment, pulled me to him for the briefest of hugs. And then they were gone.

My room was quite lovely. You'd never have known it was an institution. A non-hospital-like bed was covered in a very pretty quilt. There was a dressing table, mirror, a couple of easy chairs and a desk. Someone had even filled a vase with snowdrops, and for some reason, it was the sight of those pretty and wistful looking flowers which broke me. As soon as Matron left the room, I fell onto the bed and wept.

I felt so alone. In all the crises I'd faced, Helen had always been there for me. The fact that she hadn't seen me once since the accident or come today lay heavy on my heart. I missed her terribly.

I wrote to her, of course, but the letters were all returned unopened. I wasn't permitted to make phone calls from my beautifully decorated prison cell. The lines of communication were shut down.

To give Mother her due, she visited religiously every Wednesday. Part of me couldn't help but think she'd chosen that day on purpose. She wore the visits like a pair of shoes that are a bit too tight and she couldn't wait to remove. I always asked for news of you and Helen. I was like a fish being starved of water, but all I got were droplets. You were thriving. Helen was thriving. Everyone, it seemed, was thriving without me.

Mary came to visit once. Kind, dependable Mary who didn't ask me anything but let me weep on her shoulder until I was spent. This diminutive woman had been a huge presence in my life. Not once had she judged me or made me feel anything other than loved. Despite that, her loyalty to Mother and Daddy didn't permit her to discuss you. She simply said she wasn't to talk of it and steered the conversation in another direction. I clung to her when it was time for her to leave. She bore it very well, but eventually, she released herself and was gone. I never saw her again.

Daddy came to visit too. Not every week, and he never stayed long. Our conversation was stilted and embarrassed. Often, we didn't talk at all. Other times I cried and he simply handed me a handkerchief. I'd been at The Towers for about four weeks when Daddy came in clutching some paperwork and a suggestion for my future. It was known as the Assisted Passage Migration Scheme, but you probably know it as the Ten Pound Pom scheme. Australia set it up in 1945 to encourage people to start a new life down there. Thousands of people were leaping at the chance of a brand new beginning on the other side of the world. Daddy enthused about it. It would be a fresh start for me—a chance to wipe the slate clean and make a new life for myself.

I don't think I'd realised until then how effectively my actions had cut myself off from the family. I'd assumed that, as usual, they'd just forgive me and we'd rebuild some kind of relationship. My arrogance was breath-taking. I expected a level of compassion and forgiveness that I certainly wouldn't have extended had the shoe been on the other foot. Daddy's words brought reality crashing in. They didn't want me back. They would prefer I took myself away as far as humanly possible. It hurt.

Worse was to come. Daddy had a letter from Helen. I have kept that letter with me ever since. It has helped me to remain the person I needed to become. I have read it so many times the words are etched on my memory. In essence, Helen told me that while she loved me and always would, she could no longer run the risk of having me around you.

She wanted you to grow up in a safe and secure environment. She wanted your happiness to come before all else. Her days of covering up for me and sorting out my mistakes were over. Protecting you was her priority. I was on my own. Therefore, she felt it best for everyone if I moved away and she'd like to discuss this with me further. She would arrange to visit later in the week.

I read the last sentence with hope. It was my lifeline. I could change her mind. I'd always been able to do that. I would show her I was a different woman. I would do anything if I could just stay.

On the morning of her visit, I made sure my hair and makeup were perfect. I chose a pretty dress and, fully armed, sat down to wait. As soon as she entered the room, I knew I'd lost. She swept in like a queen and carried herself with an air of confidence I'd never seen before. This was a very different Helen to the gentle, crying creature I could normally manipulate so well. Here was a

157

lioness fighting for her cub and woe betide anyone who got in her way. In the past, my tears, tantrums and reproaches had always worn Helen down, and I'd always been able to make her see my point of view. It was a crushing blow to find myself powerless.

Helen was cool and collected. I cried and stamped my feet. Helen was rational and concise. I was incoherent and blubbering. The power shift was absolute. Never again would I hold sway over her life and her decisions.

There was no real discussion after that. She simply told me what would happen. She, Francis, the girls, Daddy and Mother would move to Scotland. I would move to Australia. This would be best for everyone. I would be able to establish a new life for myself with new possibilities. But most importantly, I would be unable to interfere in your life. This, Helen announced, would give you the best possible chance. Surely that was what we all wanted.

I would be allowed to see you one last time before I left. I was to come to the house for morning refreshments. All the arrangements for my journey, finances etc., would be taken care of. Mother even had a cousin in Perth I could stay with initially. She was, of course, wholly ignorant of the real reason for my journey to the furthest place from home. I would be welcomed as a girl who'd suffered a broken heart not once but twice and needed distraction.

That was that. My life was sewn up in a neat bundle that need never affect you again. I was to be shuffled off to the other side of the world out of harm's way. They needn't fear for my actions and their consequences again. I wanted to refuse point-blank, but in the end, I had to agree. I knew they were right. I knew myself well enough to know that if I stayed, I'd never rest until I drove a wedge between you and Helen. I'd want you to myself.

I begged Helen to tell you about me when you were twenty-one. Following a discussion with Francis, she wrote to me to tell me they'd agreed. You were to be told about me and also where I was. You would then be given the option to contact me. But it would be your decision.

The fact that you never did fills me with great sorrow. I had hoped that you would reach out to me. I looked in vain for letters in the year following your coming of age. As one year rolled into the next, I had to accept that you didn't want to hear from me, and I had to adhere to your decision. The only reason I have broken it now is because I'm dying. Oh, don't waste your sympathy on me, my darling. I'm ninety-two years old. I've lived a full and interesting life. The only regrets I have are in these letters. Please don't weep for me, Eve. I couldn't bear it.

And besides, I'm tired. My time here is done. Australia has been good to me. It's a beautiful country with beautiful people. Life here is less formal and uptight than the environment I grew up in, and it has suited my nature more. Despite the pain of leaving you behind, I have to agree with my family; Australia did give me a new life.

After a year of settling in and finding my feet, I started working at a local orphanage. Helping children has been central to my life. Abandonment guilt, no doubt. Whatever the reason, I was good at what I did.

I kept up correspondence with Daddy, and not long after starting work, I met Gregg. After a month or so, I wrote and asked Daddy to arrange the sale of Robert's house on my behalf. Gregg and I used the money to open our own orphanage on our first wedding anniversary.

Gregg was no Douglas or Robert. He was uniquely his own person. He loved me dearly but never gave into my whims. Unlike Robert, he was no 'yes man', and he had no qualms about telling me so. We rowed, and we were both stubborn. But we worked, and he treated me as an equal, not some delicate flower that needed to be protected. We were a true partnership. Gregg taught me so much about tolerance and care and it is purely down to him that I learnt to be less demanding. We were very happy together. He died ten years ago surrounded by his wife, children and grandchildren.

You have two half-siblings, a brother and a sister. They, in turn, have children and grandchildren of their own. A year or so after Gregg died, I told them about you. Oh, not the full story, just the nice palatable bits. You were a love child, and I fled the country to spare the family embarrassment. Whatever I missed out of the tale, the 'love child' was right. You were loved and you were conceived in love. I want to reassure you of that.

And I know you were loved by the Monmouths and Fenwicks. Helen sent an annual letter to update me. At first, these missives were quite cold and distant, but as time mellowed, so did the tone. She told me when you met your young man, Clive, about your marriage and subsequent children. She assured me you had a happy life. I'm glad, Eve. Leaving you behind was the most devastating thing I've been through, but I do believe it was for the best. I want you to know I have never stopped thinking about you. The memory of your little arms around my neck and your adorable giggle has stayed with me despite time and distance. You are still the last thing I think of when I go to sleep.

So there it is, Eve. My story. Not a gratifying read at times and elements of it must have been truly shocking. Please believe me, that was not my intention, but having embarked on the tale, I couldn't leave anything out. The last thing I ever wanted to do was shock or upset you, but I have undoubtedly been a master of both.

I had a long talk with my children about whether contacting you was the right thing to do after all these years. In the end, it seemed right, so I asked my son Noel to arrange the delivery of the letters to you via Daddy's old solicitors. It seems there are some things which don't change. Both Noel and Charlotte (my daughter) agreed they'd want to know if they were you. They are, of course, unaware of the full unabridged version. My deepest wish is that one day you will get to know your siblings on this side of the world. Technology makes the distance seem almost non-existent.

I know it's too late for me, and neither time nor health are on my side. But Noel and Charlotte are innocent parties in this, just as you are. The final envelope will open the door or leave it shut as per your choice.

I made so many mistakes in my early life. I was thoughtless, spoilt, arrogant and at times unbelievably selfish. The most noble and brave thing I've ever done was to leave you in Helen and Francis's care. She was a truly wonderful woman and Francis was a great man. Through our annual letters, which continued until her death, Helen and I finally reached a place of affection and love again. I know I can't ask the same from you, but I truly hope you can forgive me.

All my love,
your mother
X

CHAPTER 27

I sat for some time just holding the letter. What it had lacked in the shocking news about Robert's death, it made up for in revelations of siblings on the other side of the world.

The world which contained just Susan and I had been well and truly shaken up. Was it really just this morning when I'd been boring old Eve Gilchrist? In the following hours, I'd been swept along through highs and lows and twists and turns. It had been disorientating, dizzying and nauseating in equal measure. My emotions were in a complete muddle.

Doris's story may have concluded, but I was left with so many questions. Was she still alive, and if so, did I want to make contact? She had burst into my life and left a devastating path behind her. The family I thought I knew were a world away from the one described in Doris's account. My dear, kind parents Helen and Francis had covered up a death, lied, connived and plotted to get

Doris out of the way. They'd also lied to me, hidden the fact that my birth mother was very much still alive. Whether I would have wanted to make contact with Doris was immaterial. It was the fact they'd taken my choice away that hurt. And even more frustrating, I couldn't even tell them how this made me feel. My grandparents had taken part in the grand cover-up and plot as well—so many lies. As for Grandmother, she had taken on the role of pantomime baddy, which was so alien from the woman of my memories. I didn't know what to think of it all.

Throughout my early and mid-teenage years, I'd battled with my emotions. I'd learnt to quell the rising anger which seemed to come upon me unbidden. My family had looked on anxiously as I learnt to control myself. All that time I'd been led to believe I was behaving irrationally or in an unbecoming way when in reality, I'd merely carried on the trait of instability in my genes. It hadn't been my fault after all.

And it hadn't been our son Robert's fault either. His temper was inherited too. Poor Rob, he'd fought with the anger demon since he was very small. Thankfully, through Clive's contacts, we'd had strategies and therapists on hand to help him with varying degrees of success. Although he'd never done anything as drastic as Doris and tended to take his temper out on things, not people, it had cost him his first marriage.

His ex-wife Kirsten had tried to be patient. She'd supported him and encouraged him to attend regular anger management sessions. She'd even enrolled him in martial arts classes to give his anger a more positive outlet. I'll never forget when she rang me to say it was over. We'd cried together. She was like a second daughter to me and as much as I wanted her to give Rob another chance, I also wanted her to have a chance at happiness. When I'd gone to see Rob that night, he was sat in a sitting room which looked like a whirlwind had destroyed it.

Two years of intensive cognitive behaviour therapy and hypnotherapy had worked wonders. He'd even met his second wife in the hypnotherapist's waiting room. Rob was now more content and even-tempered than he'd ever been, and he and Kirsten were still friends of a sort. What he (and indeed me) might have done without professional help was terrifying, and it made Doris's behaviour almost easier to understand if not condone.

I realised I was still clutching the letter. I lowered it to the table and took a sip of water. Now what? After such a build-up, I felt a bit deflated that it was over.

The biggest question I needed to address now was whether Doris was still alive. If she was, did I want to make contact? I didn't know the answer. Rampant curiosity screamed yes; reach out to the woman who brought me into the world. But I wasn't sure I was emotionally ready. Ditto my half-siblings, Noel and Charlotte. In a world that had only ever bracketed Eve and Susan together, two new names were on the edge trying to get in. Were they unwelcome guests? I wasn't sure. Speaking of Susan, what on earth would she make of it all?

I rolled my shoulders and tipped my head from side to

side. A knot of tension was building between my shoulder blades and my head was moving from ache to throb. What a day! And there was still one envelope to go. It was so thin compared to the others that somehow, I just knew it wouldn't be from Doris.

I opened it and pulled out two pieces of paper. The first was an official letter from the solicitor confirming that they had been instructed by the last will and testament of Doris Elizabeth Travis to pass on the letters with their covering letter to be read last. The second piece of paper held the contact information for Noel and Charlotte.

She was dead then. I checked the letter again and yes, she'd died three months ago. I let that sink in.

Tears bubbled up only to dissipate into the room without sound. Should I weep for her? Should I feel a sense of regret or loss? Maybe I should feel angry that she'd turned my life upside down and now I couldn't even demand answers from her. Could I even process this yet?

The last question was the easiest to answer. No. Not yet. As for the rest, it would have to wait. My fragile reserve of emotional energy didn't have to consider Doris's feelings anymore. I just had to think about my siblings, and of course, Susan came first. She would always come first. I was dreading her arrival tomorrow. I don't think I could bear to sit here while she read each letter and gasped or cried in response.

I moved on impulse and pushed myself out of the chair with energy I wouldn't have thought possible.

"Clive! Clive!" I called. I arrived breathless at his study door, clutching the remaining few letters. "Are you up to date?" I burst into the room and Clive looked up. Benji ran over.

"Just, I was going to come through and get the rest. Are you ok? Any other shocks I need to prepare for?"

"No, yes, God, I don't know anymore. But I need you to read these as quickly as you can. I need to drop them all off at Susan's."

"But she's coming tomorrow. Can't it wait?"

"No! I can't sit here or pace the floor while she reads them all. I want her to come here forewarned that her sister is her cousin and that her aunt was a murderer!"

"You know, Eve, technically, it was manslaughter."

A red mist descended, and the rage welled up in me so quickly it scared me.

"Oh, stop being so bloody calm and restrained about it all, Clive. This is serious, for God's sake. However you choose to dress it up, my mother was a killer. A killer, all right. And the sooner we both accept that, the better." My voice had risen with every word. Benji whined and retreated. He squirmed up onto Clive's lap made himself into a tight little ball.

"I do accept it, Eve. Well, as much as I've had time to. And you may find me maddening, but it's true. She didn't set out to kill Robert. She didn't plan to do away with him and you have to accept that."

The seconds passed; the red mist cleared. Clive was right. I repeated my mantra 'in with calm and out with anger' several times. Doris hadn't set out to kill Robert. I had to cling onto that.

"I'm sorry, Clive, you're right about Doris. But I have to get those letters to Susan tonight. How soon can you have them finished?" Clive looked at me long and hard for a moment or two, then nodded.

"Give me half an hour."

Benji jumped off Clive's lap and padded out with me. He seemed to realise the rational Eve was back. I'd take him for a quick walk around the block. I needed to stretch, and I couldn't stand the suspense of waiting for Clive to finish. Benji was ecstatic when he saw me approach the drawer which held his lead. He bounded around my ankles, making a thorough nuisance of himself. I threw on a light jacket, shoved my keys and poo bags in my pocket and pulled the door shut behind us both.

Normally I'd have had a running commentary with Benji. I'd have also done battle every time he wanted to stop and sniff. I did neither today. My mind was in a fog, and I didn't know when it would clear. It felt good to be walking, though. I'd spent far too long sitting down today.

The first five minutes of the walk were spent getting rid of the last vestiges of my temper. My anger management techniques were being tested today, that was for sure. Once I felt the anger fully dissipate, my thoughts returned to the Summer House for some reason. Not the one at Fremell Hall...ours. I'd have to do something to exorcise it. I couldn't allow it to be sullied and I simply couldn't imagine pulling it down. It represented our life and our family. I'd spent hours in there, reading books to our children. It was strangely comforting to know that I'd passed on something nice from Doris.

I didn't know what on earth to do about Noel and Charlotte either. Did I want more siblings? Susan had been all I'd ever known. We were incredibly close. Would it even be fair to introduce new dynamics into our relationship? But I couldn't just ignore the fact that I had a half-brother and sister living in Australia. It was a place we'd never been. We'd always meant to, just never got around to it. Maybe it wasn't too late to put it on the agenda. But I was getting ahead of myself. Just because Doris had told them about me didn't mean they wanted anything to do with me. They might be quite content to carry on their lives without the introduction of Eve into the mix. The Doris-fuelled fog in my mind was getting thicker. I'd walked further than I realised and it was time to go back and drop the letters off with Susan.

"Come on, Benji, let's go home."

As always, Benji's ears pricked up at the word and he practically pulled me back to the front gate. When we got inside the house, I noticed Clive had bundled all the letters together on the table in the hall. That innocuous pile of thick, creamy paper held a staggering tale and it was one I had to pass on.

"I'll be back soon," I called. I picked up the letters and turned back to the door.

CHAPTER 28

The ignition turned and 'Night on Bald Mountain' by Mussorgsky blasted into the car. It's a compelling and emotionally charged piece, but I wasn't in the right frame of mind for it. I turned it off with fingers that shook, placed both hands on the steering wheel and inhaled deeply. The oxygen floated to the places which needed it most. A couple more breaths for good measure and I'd be ready.

The drive to Susan's didn't take long and I soon pulled up outside her house. Autopilot had got me here, but that wouldn't help with the imminent conversation. I felt rooted to the sanctuary of my car. The silly air freshener my grandson had bought me caught my eye and I stared at it as if hoping for some kind of inspiration. It was a vain hope.

The pile of torn envelopes had wobbled and spread during the journey. I was grateful for Doris's bold ordering system as I hastily put them all back in order. I couldn't sit here all night. My stomach somersaulted but I gathered myself and the letters together and climbed out of the car. The familiar squeak from the gate heralded my arrival and I barely had time to ring the bell before the door was flung wide.

"Eve! Come in, come in. I wasn't expecting you. Everything ok?" Simple words. Everyday words, but they made my lip quiver. "Eve, what on earth's the matter?"

My sister Susan reached for my hand and guided me over the doorstep. She held it tight as she ushered me through to the sitting room and into a chair. The envelopes were tucked under my arm and forced me to sit awkwardly. I piled them on the floor at my feet. Susan's curious gaze followed them.

Because Helen and Doris had been so alike, Susan and I carry shared features too. Our hair had been the same colour when we were younger, although Susan had gone grey fairly early. She now wore it cropped into a funky pixie cut. She was shorter than I and a more petite build altogether. Even middle age hadn't really added the pounds. Unlike me, she hadn't inherited the dimples. But she had got the charm in abundance. Susan was also far more gregarious than I. She loved to be part of the action or conversation. Confidence oozed from her. She was also incredibly curious, and I knew the letters would be taunting her.

"Tea?" she asked.

"No!" Susan looked surprised. "I've had a lot of tea today. Sorry, I didn't mean to snap." Get it under control,

Eve, for goodness sake, I told myself. "I can't stop long, Sue. I just wanted to leave these with you." I picked up the letters and handed them over. "They came in the post this morning. I've spent all day reading them and I need you to read them before you come tomorrow."

I sat back in the chair, feeling like a runner in a relay race. Susan was talking, no doubt asking questions about the letters, but I didn't listen. I couldn't listen. My body and brain had shut down. It was all I could do to remain upright in the chair. Surprisingly, no tears came. I was even too tired for that.

"Eve, Eve...listen to me! Can you hear me? Shall I call Clive?"

I emerged from my seclusion to see Susan standing over me. She looked scared and I hastened to reassure her.

"Sorry, love, I didn't mean to alarm you. I've had a hell of a day and I can't go into it now. I haven't got the words or the energy. I just need you to read them before you come. Will you do that for me?"

"Of course, I will!"

I knew curiosity would be eating her up. She'd barely wait for me to leave before settling down to read. I owed her a warning, at least.

"Sue, they're a bit of a shock. Actually, a lot of shock. You'll see what I mean."

Duncan popped his head around the door.

"Hi, Eve. Cuppa?"

"No thanks, I can't stop. Just a flying visit to drop something off. Sue will fill you in."

I dragged myself out of the chair and hugged Susan tightly. A quick peck on the cheek for Duncan and I was back outside heading for the car.

"See you tomorrow," I called.

Susan and Duncan waved as I pulled away. It was done. All I could do now was process my own jumbled and messy thoughts and wait for tomorrow.

This time the radio gave me 'Canon in D' by Pachelbel. I let this one play and headed for home.

CHAPTER 29

Surprisingly, I slept well. It must have been deep, though, because when I woke, my head felt fuzzy. A sleep hangover we'd always called it. I pottered around the house and studiously avoided the Summer House. My thoughts had jumped and bounced from one thing to another all morning. I was like a gnat flitting here, there and never settling for long enough on anything. I wasn't sure what the day would bring. I wasn't even sure what I wanted it to bring. I expected something but had no idea what.

I glanced at the clock—half-past twelve. Susan would be here soon. There'd been no frantic call in the night, so I had no idea how she'd be feeling or even how she'd react to me with this newfound knowledge.

Clive had taken himself and Benji off for a ramble. No doubt they'd return later, muddy but content. Without even mentioning it, Clive just knew I wanted to see Susan by myself. Although what the hell I'd say to her was a mystery. I still didn't know how I should react to the news myself. I'd cried so much the day before, yet I felt strangely calm. Almost as if the whole thing was happening to someone else and I was merely a spectator.

The doorbell intruded and I jumped. My heart and stomach seemed intent on a dance which left me feeling sick. I took a breath and went to open the door. Susan stood on the doorstep, looking shattered. The bundle of letters was held tightly between her hands. Normally she oozed style and glamour, but today she looked like she'd grabbed the first thing in her wardrobe. It was the first time I'd seen her without lipstick for a long time. It was my turn to take her hand and guide her inside.

I led her to the sitting room; I needed a change of scene from yesterday. Susan hovered as if she didn't know what to do. I pushed her gently onto the sofa and headed to the kitchen to make tea. While I prepped it, I put the soup on low. It would be fine for a while.

Susan seemed to have composed herself when I carried the two steaming mugs back into the front room. She'd removed her jacket and had obviously found a lipstick in her bag. The stack of letters lay neatly on the coffee table. The air was thick with tension. Neither of us made eye contact and the silence was only punctuated by the merciless ticking of the mantelpiece clock.

"Well."

We both said it simultaneously, exchanged a smiling glance and instinctively reached for each other. The nerves and worry seemed to dissipate. Shuddering sobs filled us both and our words tumbled out as an incoherent mess which neither of us could understand but nonetheless offered comfort to each other. After a minute, the torrent of words and tears dried up. The hug came to a natural end, and we both sat back limp and exhausted. Eventually, Susan spoke.

"Talk about skeletons in the closet!" She brushed her wet cheeks with a tissue.

"This won't change things, will it? For us, I mean?" The fear was finally voiced.

"Of course not, Eve! You're my sister and I love you. That's never going to change."

The relief washed over me. That was the one thing I'd been dreading more than anything else. I'd have to accept the news about Doris. I'd have to come to terms with the fact that my family were not as they seemed. I could even accept I had half-siblings across the other side of the world. What I couldn't have accepted was Susan rejecting me. Everything else was manageable.

"Thank God! That's the thing that's been playing on my mind. I dreaded our relationship being ruined. The thought of you not wanting to be part of my life was too much to bear."

"Well, you don't need to worry about that. I'm going nowhere."

I squeezed her hand gratefully and reached for my tea.

"Can you bear to eat something?" I asked.

"Surprisingly, yes. I couldn't face breakfast and now I'm starving."

Susan deposited her jacket on the coat stand and followed me to the kitchen. The soup smelt delicious. While I stirred it, Susan bustled around gathering bowls and buns. We sat at the table and ate.

"So, what do you want to do, Eve?"

"I'm not sure. I know Doris told Noel and Charlotte about me, but I still don't know how they'll feel if I get in touch. I'm not sure how I'd feel if I were them."

"Well, I'd be dying of curiosity," said Susan with a smile.

"No need to tell me that, love. Curiosity has always been your best friend. To be totally honest, I don't think I'm ready to decide yet. Clive thinks we should go away for a few days. Hire a cottage and just walk and talk until the plan sort of forms itself. And of course, I'll have to think about what to tell Rob and Marianne."

"There's no rush, though, is there? I think the cottage is a great idea. Get away, relax, walk Benji, drink wine in the evening sun. Sounds perfect."

"When you put it like that, I have to agree."

Susan nibbled the last of her bun, stacked the bowls and took them to the side.

"Cup of tea in the Summer House?" she asked. I shuddered.

"No! I can't even bear to look at it at the moment. Just the thought of the place makes me feel sick."

"What on earth for?"

"After what Doris did. Robert dying at her hands. It's just too awful."

"Eve, you do realise that your Summer House had absolutely nothing to do with this. What Doris did was done a long time ago and many, many miles away from here."

I placed my hands over my eyes. Susan was right. My Summer House had nothing to do with Robert's death. The logical side of my nature was screaming this loud and clear, but something was stopping me from listening. I hadn't worked out what yet.

"Look, if it makes you feel that way, maybe we should try to find Fremell Hall. Kind of exorcise the ghost of Doris if you like. Don't you have an urge to see the place anyway? We could both go."

I remembered vaguely suggesting the same thing to Clive. I hadn't given it much serious thought, but perhaps it was a good idea. Would seeing where I'd spent my first few years be a good thing? If the Summer House there was still standing, maybe I could banish the macabre thoughts I had about the one in my own garden.

"You might be right, Sue, but I can't think about it yet. I haven't got the energy and I wouldn't even know where to begin." My head was starting to throb.

"I'll do it. Leave it all to me. You know, nosing around on the internet is my thing. I'm sure it wouldn't take me long to track the place down. That's if it's still standing, of course, or worse, been converted into exclusive apartments."

I let the idea flit around my head. Susan could well be right. Perhaps I needed to see where it had happened to be able to move on. But did I really want to go back? Thankfully, nobody was saying I had to decide today. It was enough that the seed had been planted.

"I tell you what. I'll do a bit of research, and I'll find out what I can and let you know. It will be your decision after that, although I'll be popping with curiosity, you do know that don't you? Whatever you decide, I'll enjoy finding out a bit more about where I was born."

"I hadn't thought about it from your point of view. And you were actually born there, unlike me. Ok, you win. You always do. I'll leave you to your digging. But for God's sake, if you find out anything else horrific, just don't tell me!"

Susan filled the kettle and popped it back on the Aga. The pieces of the teapot still lay on a sheet of newspaper on the counter.

"What happened to the teapot?"

"Casualty of Doris. You might say I had a bit of a reaction, and if I'm totally honest, I lost my temper like I haven't done for years." Susan glanced at me. She still had memories of my childhood and teenage outbursts. She'd lost more than one toy to my anger. I smiled at her. "It was a one-off, Sue, don't worry. Anyway, I'm going to get it mended."

"Mended, that's optimistic, isn't it?"

"No, there are people who specialise in this kind of thing. It's called...Kat, Katis, Kint, oh, I can't remember. It's a Japanese technique. It's been around for centuries. They take the repair and turn the damage into part of the whole. It's kind of symbolic, I think. It seems appropriate anyway."

"Sounds like the teapot and a visit to Fremell Hall might both be part of the healing and acceptance process."

"I'll think about it, Sue. In the meantime, you research as much as you like."

"I'll start first thing tomorrow. For now, let's sort the tea."

I sat contentedly at the table watching Susan move around my kitchen as if it were her own. Our relationship would survive this. We'd had a jolt, nothing more. Whatever happened, we were still Eve and Susan, Susan and Eve. Nothing would change that. Not even Doris.

CHAPTER 30

"Come on, Eve! Are you ready?" Clive was standing by the front door, jangling his keys.

He'd been as good as his word and booked a few days in a cottage for us. The car was loaded, Benji was in the boot and Clive was keen to leave. I, on the other hand, was dithering about Doris's letters. Should I take them with me or leave them behind? Part of me just wanted to escape and pretend last week had never happened. But the other part of me knew I had to face this. I couldn't simply stuff them in a drawer for the next generation to find when the time came.

I couldn't let them eat away at my peace of mind either. My temper, so long kept under control, was growing inside me. It was hungry and seemed to feed on my every thought. Even my toes felt angry. I hadn't felt like this since before I met Clive. Frankly, it scared me. Doris had woken a monster and I would have to do my utmost to suppress it. I'd bought myself a beautiful new notebook and started an anger journal. It was something Rob had used when he'd been taming his inner rage. Although it sounded like something a teenager would use, I was amazed at how helpful I found it.

"Eve! Come on, love. Any chance we can leave today?"

I swallowed down an acid response, counted to ten and scooped my journal and the letters into my handbag. The three of us seemed joined whether we liked it or not.

"Coming! I was just getting a couple of things."

Clive locked the front door while I started the engine. As we pulled out of the drive, Clive patted my knee.

"This will do you good. We can walk, talk, not talk, just walk, whatever you like. Let's see what happens. Don't put so much pressure on yourself to get the answer right away. You've had a huge shock. Let it bed in." I knew he was right.

As the car ate up the miles and delivered us deeper into the beautiful Scottish countryside, my spirits lifted. They lifted further when I saw our destination—a cute stone cottage with a rustic drive and a lovely garden that encircled the cottage like a moat.

With a sigh, I turned the engine off and prised myself out of the driver's seat. Clive released Benji, who careered around the garden liberally watering virtually every plant and ornamental rock. We emptied the car and deposited supplies in the kitchen and cases in the charmingly decorated bedroom. With the kettle on for the inevitable cup of tea, we lost no time in putting groceries away and assigning clothes to drawers and hangers. With that all taken care of, we were ready to explore the local area.

Walking is wonderfully therapeutic. It lifts you when you are down, dazzles your senses and allows for in-depth conversation. And questions.

"How do you really feel about the letters, Eve? You've not mentioned them since."

"The million-dollar question. Honestly, I don't know. I don't know what I'm supposed to feel."

"Well, that's the point, isn't it? You have to ask how *you* feel? It's not about other people. It's about you."

I bit my lip.

"I don't know, Clive. I feel like all normal feelings have been upended. Am I supposed to be outraged or disgusted? Angry? Should I feel sad and have a sense of loss for Doris? Should I be cross with Mum and Dad for hiding this from me? And what about Grandma and Grandpa? See, it's too much. My head will explode, or I will!"

The flicker of anger was making itself felt. I clenched my fists. Clive glanced at me and seemed to feel its heat. He reached out, took one of my hands and squeezed it. I felt the anger settle.

"So, unpack those questions one by one. Just don't expect a neatly wrapped single answer."

"Right, more confusion."

"No one said it would be easy, Eve."

I knew he was right. But that knowledge didn't make it any more palatable and it certainly didn't make it any easier. The path meandered down through the trees towards a small loch. It was stunningly pretty and the sunlight only served to emphasise this.

A stony shore kissed the water. We were the only people there and the surface of the water was calm and serene, like a mirror, as Mum always used to say. I pushed that thought away as Benji plunged in, sending ripples and waves flying. We found a convenient rock to perch on and watched as the loch rocked and reeled while Benji played. Finally satisfied, he emerged and shook vigorously before lolling on the ground next to us.

The water he'd disturbed slowly recovered. It seemed almost thankful to return to its former placid state. The ripples and waves grew ever smaller until they simply disappeared. The loch was as it had been.

Could I hope for the same for me?

"Clive, what would you want to ask if you were me?"

"Firstly, you have to remember I'm not you. I only knew Helen and Francis as my in-laws, and I don't have all your childhood memories and experiences. I suppose what I'd really want to know is how it would affect me going forward. You can't change what's happened, Eve. That's already done."

Feeling restless, I left the rocky perch and walked to the edge of the loch kicking the pebbles between my feet. I found a nice flat one, and bending over, I picked it up and flicked it Ducks and Drake style into the water. It bounced two, three, four times, then sank without a trace. Only the ripples were an indication of what had gone on before.

"Let's walk, love." I stretched my hand towards Clive, and we set off along the shore.

I didn't have to find the answers today. I didn't even have to find the answers during this little break. They'd come in time, and when they were ready, so would I be.

CHAPTER 31

The few days away had done me a lot of good, and when we returned, I felt able to give some serious thought to many of the questions I'd raised. Over the coming weeks, I thought of Doris and her letters frequently. Clive and I, Susan and I and sometimes Duncan, discussed every aspect. My anger journal was teeming with words and phrases which were becoming less rage-filled and more like a general diary.

Clive and I had decided to tell our children and their partners some of the truth. They now knew I was Aunt Doris's illegitimate daughter and that she hadn't died but had, in fact, lived in Australia, where she'd gone on to have another family. I'd also had a frank discussion with Rob about Doris's anger and indeed my own. In all the years we'd been helping him fight his own demons, I'd never mentioned mine. He'd never known the angry Eve of my teenage years had existed. To hear that I and indeed his grandmother had our own battles with rage was an eye opener. Not surprisingly, he was quite upset

I'd never told him when he was growing up. My constant reassurances that I understood what he was going through had fallen on deaf ears at the time. Now he knew I really had understood, and I realised I should have told him sooner. Maybe he'd have felt less isolated by his anger if he'd known he wasn't the only one. We'd talked more openly than we had for years, so although Doris had caused much upset, she had also been the catalyst for a better understanding between me and my son.

As for the rest of the immediate family, Rob and Marianne's grown-up children also knew about Doris being my mother. Everyone had accepted it serenely and with a nonchalance that was almost insulting. I'd been worrying and worrying how they'd take the news and they had been distinctly unworried or bothered. Sometimes it's hard to explain how quickly society has moved on in the last forty years. What would have been shocking to one generation is water off a duck's back to another. Of course, they didn't yet know about Robert's death, and I was still undecided about whether or not to tell them. I had to decide if that was a burden they really needed. Maybe once I'd visited Fremell Hall, I'd have a better idea.

Susan and Clive had both persuaded me this was a good idea. A way of sealing off the past and, more importantly, a way to make our own Summer House my little piece of heaven once more. I still hadn't been in since the day Doris's letters arrived. Clive had done his best to tempt me with nightcaps and starry skies, but I'd remained adamant. I really hoped the trip away would free me from my distaste of the place.

Susan had taken care of all the arrangements for our visit to Fremell Hall. The charm and charisma that Grandmother had passed onto Doris had made its way to Susan as well. People had always been tripping over themselves to assist her. The current owners of the Hall were no exception. Following a day or so of digging, she'd made contact. A flurry of emails had assured her they'd be delighted to welcome us back to our former family home. The visit was set for two weeks' time.

In the meantime, Clive had been researching Kintsugi and had parcelled up the pieces of the decimated teapot before posting them off. Life had continued with Zumba and visits from the children and grandchildren. On the surface, it was back to normal service as usual.

Underneath it all, I was a bit of a wreck. The well-ordered and ordinary life of Eve Gilchrist had been well and truly shaken up. It seemed strange to me that people couldn't tell just by looking at me. Couldn't they see that my mother had killed my father and tried to abduct me? Didn't it screech from every pore of my skin? Apparently not. Interactions with friends, family and members of the community continued with staggering normality.

I wish I knew what to do so I could feel normal too. Jostling with everything else were thoughts about Noel and Charlotte. Would they really be interested in a half-sister thrust into their lives at this stage? Surely, they'd be fine without me. And wasn't I fine without them? It had been Susan and I for so long I wasn't sure I needed anyone else. Having another sister was one thing I could almost imagine getting my head around, but a brother! Clive's brothers and Duncan were the closest I had, and I wasn't sure I needed any others. Doris hadn't told them the whole story anyway. Once again, I'd be left with the burden of knowledge.

The letter with their contact details lay on my bedside table. Several times I'd taken it out of the envelope and looked at the information. One morning, I'd even done a bit of my own nosing on the internet. I'd Googled both their addresses. Not that they told me anything. Their vast island on the other side of the world seemed as distant as the moon. Charlotte had a Facebook page which I'd tried to look at. Security settings allowed me a tiny glimpse and nothing more. I wondered if, like me, her grandchildren had set her up on social media, making sure everything was safe and secure.

I could have a whole flurry of nieces and nephews and their respective offspring in my new family bubble. My mind boggled at the thought of it all. Several weeks had passed since Doris's letters had arrived and they'd passed in a blink. I still had no idea what to do. But Charlotte and Noel's contact details served as a nightly reminder that I'd have to do something. Susan and I were off to Oxfordshire soon and I'd promised myself the decision would be finalised when I got back.

Until then, life still had to go on and Benji still needed exercise. Our daily walks had become little bits of therapy for me since Doris's big reveal. He was a very good listener and absolute in his discretion. As soon as I went to the cupboard to retrieve my walking shoes, he knew he was in for a treat. His little, stumpy tail wagged ferociously, and he made that funny little noise which Clive and I think means 'Hurry up Mum, I'm ready!'.

"Come on, then. Let's go."

I clipped Benji's lead on, stuffed yet more poo bags in my pocket and headed for the door.

At the last minute, I decided to take Benji further afield and ensconced him in the car. There was a lovely isolated little hill walk about a ten-minute drive away, and it was just what I needed. The sky was a bit overcast and it looked like rain would settle in later, but we'd probably get around the four-mile loop in time.

Released from the boot of the car, Benji ran hither and thither as I rambled on behind him. After a few minutes, the path started its incline to the summit and I switched to low long strides to ease my way up. Thoughts of my parents and grandparents chased through my mind. Their behaviour, so out of character with everything I thought I knew about them, was still baffling me. I'd always considered our family to have a 'good' moral compass. We were rule followers and law-abiding citizens. The thought that they'd covered up a murder or manslaughter to give it the correct term, however accidental, was still staggering.

My breath became more laboured as the path became a little steeper. This part of the walk was truly invigorating and I arrived at the top gasping. The view was spectacular on a clear day, but even under cloud, it was a joy to behold. Today though, it didn't touch me as it normally would.

As I stood there recovering from the climb, I suddenly felt an overwhelming sense of hurt and anger wash over me. I wanted to talk to my parents and grandparents. I wanted to tell them of my anger and my utter disbelief at the part they'd played in my history. I needed them to know I did not approve of their actions and I didn't understand. As for Doris! No coherent words sprang to mind, and no eloquent sentences could convey my feelings. So, I simply opened my mouth and screamed. An anguished, frustrated, hurt-filled scream, some might say roar, gushed out of me.

It didn't last long, a few seconds at the most, but it left me drained. I lowered myself to the ground and stared unseeing over the surrounding countryside. Benji was hovering around me. My vocal torture had unnerved him and he pressed himself against me then tried to climb on my knee.

"It's all right, boy. I'm ok." I stroked his wiry fur and pulled his ear gently through my fingers. "I'm ok. I'm ok." I'm not sure how many times I said it or indeed how long we sat there.

In the end, it was my hips that forced me to move. Sitting on the ground with a dog on my lap was making them protest. I moved my legs and Benji got off. It took effort and a bit of ungainly movement, but I lurched somehow back to my feet. I felt exhausted, but thankfully, the anger and hurt had dissipated. I wasn't sure if I felt happier or more resolved just yet, but I definitely felt calmer. Maybe there's more to this scream therapy than I'd given it credit.

I didn't have the energy to complete the usual circuit, and somewhat to Benji's surprise, we went back to the car the way we'd come. There were still wisps of cloud overhead, but the heavier rain clouds had lifted and moved on. I took it as a sign of hope.

CHAPTER 32

The journey down the tedious motorway network had dragged. We'd chatted, called out the answers to Pop Master, switched to classical music and sat in companionable silence. If it hadn't been for the dread that I'd packed along with everything else, I'd have been looking forward to it. It felt a bit strange to be travelling without Clive, but it had been years since Susan and I had been away, just the two of us. Like everything else to do with this trip, I'd been happy to leave the organisation to her. All I'd had to do was drive. So far, the weather was being kind and I was glad. The thought of accomplishing this visit in damp and dismal conditions didn't appeal.

The sat nav assured us our destination was coming up on the left. I indicated and turned onto a neat car park area in front of Rose Cottage. The bed and breakfast was aptly named as the trellis surrounding the front door was heavy with gorgeous blooms. Deep corals and pinks merged with yellows and peaches, like a sunset around the entrance. A white-washed cottage with a thatched roof couldn't have screamed more English countryside if it had tried. It was chocolate-box perfect and very lovely.

"Sue, it's beautiful!" I enthused.

"I thought you'd like it. As soon as I saw it, I knew it was the right place."

We retrieved our pull-along cases from the boot and decided that carrying them would be better than dragging them across the less than forgiving gravelly surface. The solid oak front door stood open. It led into a stone-flagged entrance hall where the reception desk and a tall man awaited us.

"Good afternoon, I'm Edward. Welcome to Rose Cottage." Slick and professional Edward gave us some forms to fill in, a map for the local area and our keys. "You can't miss your rooms, ladies. Top of the stairs and turn left. Yours are the only ones on that side of the house."

We thanked him and climbed the somewhat uneven staircase. The wood gleamed with hundreds of years' worth of human touch and polish. I bet these walls had some tales to tell. Whether they'd be as strange as my own was anyone's guess.

"Which number are you, Eve?"

Susan's question cut through my thoughts. I looked at my key and a bold number six stood out. The door on the left-hand side of the corridor was mine.

"Shall we unpack then go downstairs for a cup of tea?"

"And a bite to eat as well, Eve. I'm hungry, aren't you?"

"I know I should be, but I guess I'm a bit out of sorts with everything. I can't quite believe we're here."

"Trust me, you'll feel better for some food. A few biscuits and a service station muffin is no way to keep yourself going."

"Give me half an hour, then knock when you're ready."

I closed the heavy wooden door behind me, heaved a sigh and glanced around the room. The walls were crooked, and the beams and floors seemed a little bit out of alignment, but this only added to the overall charm. Two deep windowsills which supported the small windows held vases of roses. They filled the room with a wonderful fragrance. Something snatched at my memory but was gone in a flash. Had there been a rose garden at Fremell Hall? Had I played amongst its heavy perfume? I frowned with concentration, but it eluded me.

For the past few weeks, I'd been operating on autopilot. Smiles for the children, grandchildren and our little great-granddaughter, walking Benji, talking to Clive and Susan, heart to hearts with Rob. I'd done all of them in a sort of daze. Now I was in a room by myself where nobody had any expectations of me. I moved towards the bed and perched on the edge. That's when the tears started. Not gasping, gusty sobs, these simply rolled down my cheeks and dripped onto my clasped fingers. I was too exhausted to wipe them away.

This trip was the culmination of weeks of emotion and reaction. And weeks of trying not to show it. Only Clive and, to a lesser degree Susan, had had to endure the emotional rollercoaster. They'd seen the daily battles with my insecurities and fears. I'd pinned so much expectation on this trip. What if it left me in a worse place than before? Maybe I wouldn't find the answers. I had to face the very real possibility that the closure I was seeking may simply not exist.

Susan and Clive had done all they could in the run-up to the trip. They'd listened, advised and encouraged me. And through talking to them, it had dawned on me that the person I really wished to make my peace with was my father, Robert. He had been the true victim of this sorry mess. I was merely the product of it. Robert had had his life cut short and his passing hadn't even been marked. For all I knew, the police still held him on the Missing Person's list. And that was assuming such lists even lasted this long. The fact that there was no final resting place to visit had also preyed on my mind. All I had to go on were fragments of clues in Doris's letters. I'd convinced myself that the quarry must have been used as a convenient place. The fact that it had been my kind and gentle dad who'd done the disposing was something I could still barely comprehend.

I planned to visit the quarry tomorrow. Susan didn't know this yet. I glanced at my watch. I'd been sitting on the bed for twenty minutes. Susan would be knocking on the door soon. My tears had finally stopped and dried in salty tracks down my face. I fished my wash bag out of my case and attempted to repair the damage. The water felt cool on my flushed cheeks. I glanced at my face in the bathroom mirror. God, Doris had aged me. I looked careworn and anxious. A dab of lipstick would do the job.

I was never as well-groomed as Susan, but I took some pride in my appearance. With little time left, I dragged my clothes out of the case and put them away without my usual thought or care. My shoes went on the handy 'shoe mat' by the door, and my journal, Doris's letters and a separate envelope for Robert went onto the bedside table. That would have to do, for now. I could refine the tidying later on.

I changed my travel-weary top for something a bit more presentable and patted my hair back into place. With my handbag over my shoulder, I opened the door. It was time to tell Susan of my plans for tomorrow. And about the letter.

CHAPTER 33

Not surprisingly, Susan had had a complete change and had touched up her hair and makeup as well. She always made me feel slightly scruffy and under-groomed. We made our way down the stairs to ask Edward about food options.

"Stocks Tavern. It's the local pub and it's a must. Their homemade pies are the best for miles around. It's a jealously guarded recipe that's stayed with the pub from landlord to landlord or landlady, of course. You're lucky it's mid-week, or you wouldn't have a hope of getting a table."

"Is it far?" I asked.

"Half a mile or so up the road. Turn left out of the car park and keep going. If you get to the church, you've gone too far."

The walk was a welcome relief after the hours in the

car. The afternoon sun had mellowed to a warm glow, and it felt good on our backs. Edward was right; we couldn't miss the pub. There it was, in all its Old English splendour, a rambling, low-roofed building at least three or four centuries old. Every inch of it seemed to exude a warm welcome to weary travellers.

We opted to eat on the modern decking area, overlooking a frankly magnificent garden. We had it pretty much to ourselves, which was just as well given what we'd be discussing. As we sat down, I wondered if Mum and Dad or Doris had ever come here. Fremell Hall was just three miles away, so it was a distinct possibility. Although, of course, Helen and Doris would never have had lunch here by themselves. That was simply not done by ladies back then. A lot of things had changed over the years. I wished Dad was here. He'd have undoubtedly had a tale to tell about the place if they had visited. I felt a pang of regret for all the questions that would now remain unanswered. The little snippets of history that get passed on to the next generation with nostalgia were lost to us. We'd never know if the famous pie had existed then or been a favourite of the Marvellous Monmouths.

I shook myself free of such thoughts and concentrated on the menu. Steak and mushroom or chicken and leek. They both sounded delicious. As usual, I'd leave the decision until the moment of ordering. I plumped for steak and mushroom.

"Ok, out with it," said Susan as soon as our order had been taken and the waitress had retreated. "You're like a cat on hot bricks."

"Sorry, nerves, I guess. It's not every day you plan to see the place where your mother killed your father. Look, Sue, I have a couple of things I need to discuss about tomorrow. What time are they expecting us again?"

"10.00 am, Tony has a call to take in the afternoon. He's a historian doing research for a big project."

"And you've definitely asked about the Summer House? We can go and see it?"

"Yes, don't panic, that's all sorted. I explained it had been an important element of your childhood and you were keen to see it."

"Well, that's one way of putting it, I suppose!"

"The main thing is they are very happy to oblige. Charles uses it as an art studio now."

"There's somewhere else I want to go as well—the quarry."

"The quarry? What on earth for?"

The waitress returned with our drinks and effectively stopped the conversation in its tracks. We'd both opted for gin and tonic with a glass of water. I took a grateful sip of both.

"It was just something Doris mentioned in her letters that made me think that's where Dad put the body. It would make sense. The entrance was through their land."

"But we have no proof of this," exclaimed Susan. She looked genuinely shocked. "We don't even know how close to the Summer House it is."

"Exactly, which is why I want to see."

"But I've not got the right footwear for tramping over fields to a quarry."

"Are you seriously telling me that in the vast collection of shoes you've brought with you, you haven't got so much as a pair of trainers?"

"I imagined us sipping tea in the drawing room, not battling uneven pathways. Eve, I wish you'd told me!"

"It didn't even occur to me that you wouldn't bring one pair of sensible shoes. Look, you can borrow my trainers. I've got another pair of flats I can wear."

The waitress was back once again with our food and the smell was mouth-watering. I suddenly realised how very hungry I was. I laid the lovely, thick serviette across my lap and pushed my knife through the gorgeous pastry topping. The aroma was mouth-watering. I was looking forward to this.

"Do you really think the quarry is where Robert ended up?" Susan was starting on her pie with gusto as well.

"I don't know, but it seems like the obvious place. Easier than digging a hole." I winced at how callous I sounded. "I'll never know for sure, but something is telling me I'm right."

"How come he's never been found then? Aren't these quarries used by divers for training and practice?"

"I thought about that, but if the quarry is only accessible across private land, that would explain it. It makes another case for it being the right location."

"Well, if you are so set on it, I suppose there's no harm in looking. Anything else you want to look at tomorrow?"

"Not look at exactly, but there is something else I want to do." Susan's fork stopped mid-way to her mouth. She looked directly at me and raised an eyebrow. "I've written a letter."

Susan lowered her knife and fork completely.

"Who to?"

"To Robert. I feel he's the one person I need to make my peace with. Mum and Dad gave me, both of us, a good life. Whatever they did and kept from me was because they believed it was the best thing. I suppose they were trying to protect me. As for helping Doris, who knows what either of us would have done in the same situation, Sue. It's easy to be noble and morally superior from a distance, but until you're in a crisis, none of us knows how we'll act."

"And Doris?" Susan returned to her pie.

"Doris. The hours I've spent thinking about Doris! She made her own way in life, that's for sure. Her actions, however shocking, haven't impacted negatively on my life since Mum and Dad told me I wasn't theirs. For the last fifty-odd years, I've bumbled along quite nicely. I don't have anything to hold a grudge for. As Clive said, I can't dwell on what she did then, only on how it could alter me going forward."

"So why Robert?"

"Robert has been missing for nearly seventy-three years. No tombstone, no flowers, no family to mark his birthdays or passing. He's been well and truly abandoned. I feel it's time to make up for that. From what I read, he was a decent man and he deserves some kind of memorial. That's why I've written him the letter."

"I can see how that might help you, Eve, but what will you do with it?"

"I want to read it to him, then burn it and throw the ashes to the wind."

Susan blinked. She took a restorative sip from the balloon glass containing her gin and tonic.

"Right. So in Tony and Charles's garden, who we haven't met, by the way, you want to set fire to a letter and leave bits of ash on their beautiful lawn. Eve, I don't think this will work. How on earth do you expect to do that? Were you just going to ask, 'Hey Charles, you don't mind if I burn this and throw it around your studio, do you?'"

Susan drank her remaining gin and set the glass down with a sharp tap.

"Of course not. I want to do it by the quarry. I absolutely feel that it's the right place. I can't imagine Tony or Charles wanting to come there with us. It should be perfectly quiet."

"I have to admit I'm slightly relieved that you don't have the Summer House in mind. But what if we can't get to it, or worse still, there's a team-building exercise going on and the place is awash with corporate types in wetsuits."

"Susan, please stop trying to put barriers in the way. You've asked what I want to do and I've told you. If it has to be changed on the hoof, then so be it. Either way, that letter will be read and burnt, and the ashes scattered somewhere to honour that poor man whose only mistake was to love my psychotic mother." I took a ragged breath and finished my gin.

"Ok, ok. You've obviously given this a lot of thought."

"Thought! I've done nothing but think about Doris, Robert and these wretched letters since they arrived. I want some kind of closure. I'm stuck in limbo at the moment."

Susan's hand reached across the table and took mine.

"Do you want to show me the letter?"

"I don't know. I'd like you to be there when I read it, but I don't know if I want you to see it first. Does that sound daft?"

"No dafter than anything else we've dealt with in the last couple of months. If you want this as some kind of send-off for Robert, keep it until tomorrow. It will seem more poignant and ceremonial that way. Do you want to take some flowers as well?"

"Do you know, I hadn't even thought of that. That would be nice. I'll see if I can get some in the morning. I don't think I can decide anything more today."

"We'll sort it tomorrow, don't worry. Now is there anything else you need to warn me about, or shall we finish these delicious pies and have more gin?"

"Nothing else, I promise. Pie and gin it is."

CHAPTER 34

The birds twittered outside my window and the sound of a hefty door closing heralded the morning. I stretched and was amazed to actually feel refreshed. Voicing my plan to Susan had helped and clarified in my head that it was the right thing to do. I'd also told Clive about the letter on the phone last night. Like Susan, he'd offered to hear it and so I'd read my words for Robert to the love of my life by soft lamplight in a cosy bedroom. It had been a bit wobbly and a bit teary at times, but it had left me with a feeling of calm.

I checked the time on my phone and was shocked to see it was 8.00 am. Generally, I'm awake by 6.30 am, so it hadn't even occurred to me to set an alarm. I couldn't remember the last time I'd slept in so late. I eased myself out of the bed and hastened to the bathroom as fast as my newly awoken legs would let me. I was supposed to be meeting Susan for breakfast in half an hour. There would be no time for the leisurely bath I'd anticipated. Instead, it was all hands to the deck to ensure I was vaguely presentable. I was just brushing my hair when she knocked on the door. I pulled it open and apologised.

"Sorry, I slept in. I'm just about ready."

"Do you need a few minutes? I can wait downstairs."

"No, don't worry. I'll do the finishing touches after we've eaten."

Edward greeted us at the bottom of the stairs and led us to the dining area. As expected, the tables were laid with beautiful tablecloths and crockery. Vases of fresh flowers completed the effect. It reminded me about Susan's suggestion of flowers for Robert. I didn't want a whole bunch, just a single bloom would do. I'd ask Edward about a local florist when we'd finished.

Breakfast was delicious, and I tackled it with enthusiasm.

"Did you sleep ok?" asked Susan.

"Surprisingly, yes! Better than I have done for months, actually. You?"

"Mmm, a bit hit and miss. I suddenly find I'm quite nervous about today. We're going back to our roots and I'm not sure how I feel about it."

"We'll get through it, Sue. Let's just pretend we're two old dears on a trip down Memory Lane. Our lane is just a bit bumpier than some. I actually feel quite positive about it."

"I'm supposed to be comforting you, not the other way around."

"You have comforted me. I couldn't have done this without you or Clive. Telling you about the letter has made me feel far better than you can know."

With the last piece of toast eaten and the last sip of tea drunk, we made our way to the entrance hall. Edward was back behind the desk and I went to speak to him.

"I just wondered, is there a florist in the village?"

"Not today, I'm afraid. She's always closed on Thursdays. The nearest one is six miles up the road or so. Was it for something specific?"

"Oh no, well yes. I just wanted a single flower for a tribute."

"Well, if a single rose will do, you are very welcome to one of ours."

"No, honestly, I couldn't," I stammered with embarrassment.

"Please, I insist."

He opened a drawer in the desk and retrieved a small but obviously sharp pair of secateurs. He moved towards the door and beckoned us to follow. Maybe he did this for lots of guests.

"Now, let me see." He ran his fingers over the petals

before hovering over a deep coral one that was just emerging from its bud. With a snip, he handed it to me and turned back to the roses. A dusky pink bloom and then a yellow rose were also snipped.

"One for you, one for your sister and one for your tribute." He handed the roses to Susan and me.

"Thank you. That's very kind of you."

"Not at all. As you can see, we have plenty."

Susan had already secured her yellow rose with the brooch on her jacket. I'd sort mine in a minute and kept hold of both flowers carefully between my hands.

"Have a lovely day, ladies. Do you want me to book you anywhere for tonight's dinner? The Indian restaurant at the other end of the village is very good."

"Sounds wonderful," said Susan. "Could you book us a table for seven-thirty?"

"My pleasure." Edward returned to his desk, put the secateurs away and noted our request.

Susan and I returned to our rooms to collect everything we needed for the day. Doris's letters, including the photograph of us all and my letter to Robert, were already in my handbag. I wrapped the coral rose in a tissue and placed it gently in the main body of the bag. I glanced in the mirror. For some reason neither Susan nor I had discussed, we'd opted for fairly formal attire. Think Mother of the Bride minus the hat and you'll get the picture. I'd chosen a floral print dress in various shades of pink with a navy jacket. The dusky pink rose was just right and I attached it with a safety pin I'd found lurking in the bottom of my bag. Whether we'd meant to or not, we'd channelled the Marvellous Monmouths. I smoothed my jacket and cast a final glance at my appearance. I was satisfied.

I picked up my trainers and spare sensible shoes to pop in the boot of the car and stepped into the corridor just as Susan did the same.

She looked at me and simply said: "Ready?"

CHAPTER 35

Neither of us spoke on the short journey to Fremell Hall. The sat nav punctuated the silence with forceful instructions. I couldn't tell you what we passed. There were a lot of country roads and green rolling fields, and we definitely meandered through another two cute as you like villages. When the strident voice announced our imminent arrival, my senses seemed to snap back into place. I wanted to take it all in. This was the very road Doris had driven down when she'd tried to take me. I must have driven past the exact spot where she crashed the car without realising. The past hovered on my shoulder as I checked my mirror, indicated and turned right onto the driveway. I drew the car to a halt.

"Here goes." I reached for Susan's hand and she squeezed it.

"It feels so odd to think that we once lived here, doesn't it? Well, I suppose I didn't really. What was I, six months old when we left?"

"Something like that. Let's see what Fremell Hall has in store for us." I put the car into gear and pressed the accelerator.

The gravel crackled and popped deliciously under the tyres. Sturdy trees were evenly spaced along the avenue and we glimpsed what looked like a wood over to the left. At the end of the drive, it opened out into a spacious oval in front of the house. I stopped the car and cut the engine.

With cream walls and wide shallow steps leading up to a front door surrounded by columns, it was unmistakeably Georgian. The symmetrical sash windows looked down upon us. It was a very attractive and well cared for house. There was a path off to the right to what I imagined was the stable block. We swung open our respective doors and got out. For a few seconds, neither Susan nor I moved.

We both lived in nice but normal houses. To think we'd once lived in all this splendour was alien. How had Grandma and Grandpa adapted? It must have been such a shock for them. Mum and Dad had never once mentioned that this was the lifestyle they'd known and left behind. The letter Doris had sent about the tax and death duties really brought it home. Although Grandma and Grandpa had lived in a fairly large house which we'd regarded as 'posh' it seemed tiny compared to Fremell Hall. I wasn't sure how I'd have felt in their circumstances. It would be like Clive and I selling up to live in a caravan. Did they genuinely have no regrets or had the relief of getting away from here and not being saddled with crushing debt make up for it?

"Goodness," said Susan, "it's terribly grand."

"It's very nice but give me our homes any day. The cleaning and heating alone must be horrendous."

"Ever practical Eve! Come on. We can't stand on the drive all day."

I locked the car and we crunched to the steps. I reached out to the old-fashioned bell with shaking fingers and pushed. We didn't have long to wait before the door was opened by a well-groomed man in his early fifties dressed head to toe in monochrome.

"Hello, you must be Eve and Susan. I'm Charles. Do come in, although it feels a bit strange to be inviting you into your old home." He had a charming smile.

"It's been a long time since we've lived here, so please don't worry. We're very grateful you agreed to us coming down." My voice was surprisingly steady.

"It's a pleasure. It was all so intriguing."

My God, if only he knew!

Once through the front door, the hallway opened and soared up to an ornate ceiling. The flags underfoot were black and white and laid out like a chequerboard. A beautiful staircase clung to the right-hand side of the hall and led up to the floor above. Everything looked immaculate.

Charles led us through a door on the left—the

drawing room. A hint of the past assailed me again before disappearing off like a wood sprite. Unsurprisingly the room was tastefully decorated with sympathy for the original features but a clever nod to contemporary style. At the far end, in front of french windows which opened onto a terrace, another man sat elegantly on a chaise longue. He got to his feet as soon as we entered and made his way over. In complete contrast to Charles, he wore a splendidly colourful suit. I was glad we'd dressed up. This must be Tony. Strange that he, the historian, should be the one so lavishly dressed, whereas Charles, the artist, was understated. Maybe his works of art were full of colour instead.

"Susan, Eve, this is my partner, Tony. Tony, this is Susan and Eve, who used to live here."

"It's lovely to welcome you here. Tea?"

We both accepted. Charles left the room and Tony directed us towards the seating area.

"The tea won't be long. We have a lady who comes and takes care of us during the day. Between an artist and a historian, we can forget about mundane things like eating and drinking if we're not careful. Please, take a seat."

I perched myself on one of the beautiful sofas and tried to relax. I wondered how to open the proceedings, but Tony breached the gap with ease.

"So, when did your family leave here?"

Susan threw me a quick glance and thankfully took over the proceedings.

"We moved out in 1952, and as far as we know, the house had been in our family since it was built in the earlyish part of the nineteenth century. We don't really know much more than that."

"Well, as it happens, I can help fill in some of the gaps. History is my thing and I've been doing a bit of digging."

I felt my heart sink and my stomach do cartwheels. I hoped my face wasn't revealing how uncomfortable this information was making me feel. Tony's next words only made matters worse.

"I'm sure you'll understand that with my heritage I wanted to be sure that the house hadn't been paid for by the blood of too many slaves. I'm a realist, so I knew there'd be some less than savoury elements of the house's history. It's impossible to escape that when you are buying property like this. I just didn't want to live here if it had belonged to a family who'd taken delight in the trade or owned hundreds of slaves."

I couldn't find the right words in response to this. What on earth could I possibly say? I looked at Susan and she seemed similarly taken aback though thankfully, she managed to speak.

"So, what did you discover?"

Charles returned at that point carrying a tea tray and a folder clasped tightly under his arm. The tray he deposited on the ornate coffee table and the folder he gave to Tony with an affectionate smile.

"I thought you might need this."

"Ah yes, my notes and research. Mind like a sieve when it comes to everyday things. Now let's see what we have here."

While Charles poured and distributed the tea, Tony opened the folder and pulled out a comprehensive bundle of papers. I was starting to feel quite sick. What on earth would he have found out? Slave traders! Could it get any worse?

"Ah yes, here we are. The first Monmouth bought the land and built the house in 1826. His name was Alfred Monmouth and he was something big in tea."

"Well, we certainly drink enough of it!" I said with a shaky laugh.

"He lived here with his wife, Emma. That's how they named the hall, actually. Emma and Alfred became Fremell Hall with a judicial placing or misplacing of a letter or two. Anyway, his son George inherited next and carried on the family business and passed it on in turn to his son Alfred. Alfred never married and his cousin, another George, I'm guessing that's your branch of the family, inherited. From there, it passed to his son William and then another William who I imagine must have been your grandfather."

"We had no idea about the family business. Does that

mean they ran Tea Clippers across the seas?" I was starting to become a little more interested now.

"That's right. These ships were much faster and would have ensured a bigger profit. Tea was big business and only the very wealthy could afford it. Did you know it was taxed at 119 percent? Tea smuggling was rife."

"Tony, I'm not sure they need the complete history of the world. More tea, ladies? The tax is far more reasonable these days." Charles took our cups and refilled them.

"I'm guessing your grandfather didn't tell you much about the family history then?"

"No, we know nothing about it. We knew the family had been wealthy and that death duties had pretty much stopped them in their tracks. We had no idea how they'd actually made their money." I took a breath before asking the next question.

"So, it was mostly tea they transported then, not people?"

"Yes, tea was the main commodity, but inevitably there were people too. I've made some comprehensive notes about that. It doesn't make for pretty reading, as you can imagine. But we can't bury our heads and ignore the facts. Thousands and thousands of men, women and children were sold into servitude and treated worse than animals. Humanity owes it to them to learn about the horrors, even though it's something that was brushed aside for years. We simply can't pretend these things didn't happen. On the other hand, neither can we hold ourselves accountable for our forefathers' actions. It's how we learn from it and live now and in the future that matters. You'll see more detail about this in my notes, but to reassure you, the Monmouths dealt very little in the transport of humans and were quick to turn their back on it following Wilberforce's bill. Though, of course, they accepted payment for the loss of their 'goods'."

More shame to add to the family name. I shivered and Susan looked horrified. It was awful to think that members of our family, our ancestors, had contributed to the enslavement of human beings just because of the colour of their skin. This was something I'd have to educate myself on once I'd dealt with Doris. I was woefully ignorant.

Susan and I reached for our teacups to cover the moment of shame, embarrassment and unease. Yet again, it was Tony who moved the conversation on.

"Do you know why your family moved? If it were me, I'd never have left."

Such a simple and reasonable question, but following Tony's revelations of the Monmouth past, it seemed like yet another hurdle to leap. A cold sweat of fear passed over me. I hoped I wasn't going to faint on their exquisite rug. I swallowed.

"Er, no, we never really knew. I think the family money ran out. It happened to a lot of families back then. We've been in the Scottish Borders ever since." I hoped my cheeks weren't as flushed as I imagined them to be.

This was excruciating. What a terrible idea to come and drink tea with the past. Tony and Charles were far too polite to remark on the state of my face either way, but I was relieved when the next question came.

"I suppose you'd like to look around the house. I don't think the layout has changed too much since your day. We've left all the original features well alone. Apparently, the people who owned the place after your family, I think their name was Fallows, wanted to modernise it, but they didn't own it for long enough to make any real change. I think they lost all their money too, bad investments, I believe. I must research that next." Tony took our cups and stacked them on the tray.

Was it wrong of me to feel a sense of satisfaction on Doris's behalf that Margaret's reign at Fremell Hall had been short-lived? I chased the uncharitable thought away and fished in my bag for the photograph of Doris, myself and Susan.

"This is the only photograph we have of us here at the house. Can you work out where it was taken?" I held the photograph out and Charles took it and peered at it. Tony stood next to him, and together they turned to look at the fireplace on the opposite side of the room.

"I would say it's here, wouldn't you, Tony?"

"It certainly looks like the mantelpiece in here. I don't think it would be the dining room and it's definitely not the study."

Susan and I stood as one and moved over to join

them. Our parents, grandparents, and indeed all our ancestors way back to Alfred and Emma, had stood in this very room in front of this very mantelpiece. A strong wave of déjà vu washed over me and I could almost picture it as it had been when I was a child. A circular table with miniature cups and saucers. Trusty old Teddy and Dolly sitting on chairs next to me. A beautiful lady with a melodic laugh. The sun shining through the tall glass windows. I staggered back and Susan caught my arm.

"Are you all right, Eve?"

"Oh yes, sorry, I just had a very clear memory of being in this room. Could I possibly use your bathroom? I feel a little strange."

Tony and Charles were concerned, and I was ushered across the hallway to a thoroughly modern toilet the size of a small bedsit. I ran cold water over my wrists and took some deep breaths. My God, I could feel her here. I could feel all the Monmouths in the very bricks around me. I still wasn't sure if coming here was a good idea, but I had to cling to what Tony had said, *'We can't hold ourselves accountable for our forefathers' actions. It's how we live now and in the future that matters.'* I turned off the taps and used the facilities. I took some steadying breaths and did my best to restore my appearance with my trusty lipstick. It was time to return to the drawing room. Susan, of course, had utterly charmed them and the sound of laughter welcomed me into the room.

"So sorry, everyone. It was just a little overwhelming being back here."

"Not at all," said Charles. "It can't be every day you return to your ancestral home. Susan was just saying you should get a photograph of you both in front of the mantelpiece now."

I stood with Susan as Charles captured our historic visit. I hoped my face looked less like a beetroot.

"Now, are you ready for the tour? And please feel free to take as many photos as you like."

The rooms were well-proportioned and all tastefully decorated. Modern touches in the form of bold and bright paintings lifted the walls and made them sing. I wondered if they were Charles's own work. After the downstairs rooms were inspected and duly cooed over, we trod the carpeted stairs to the upper floor. These were the very stairs Doris would have carried me up in her arms. She'd have continued along the corridor to one of the bedrooms. It would have been filled with my toys, books and dresses. The landing outside would have borne witness to Helen and Doris warring over who attended to my needs. I wondered which one it could be. I also wondered which had been Doris's room, the place she'd retreated to following Douglas's death. It was impossible to know.

There were eight bedrooms in total, although not all of them were in use as such. One was a gallery of sorts filled with historical artefacts and one was a music room. I wondered how they could bear to rattle around such a huge house, just the two of them. It was splendid but not for me.

"And now to the heart of every home...the kitchen. Via the servants' stairs, of course." Tony smiled and led the way.

And just like that, we were in another world. The world of domestic life. The cavernous kitchen had been modernised, but a huge wooden table still filled the middle of the floor.

"This is the original table, apparently. Luckily for us, none of the previous owners parted with it. And we just couldn't get rid of it. It's a fabulous piece of wood. We had the new kitchen designed around it. This is where your meals would have been prepared when you lived here."

"Yes, Mary cooked them." I'd spoken out loud without realising. "I do remember being in here. I used to sit at the table and help Mary make cakes. She'd give me a little pile of sultanas to count. She came with us to Scotland, you know. She died not long after my grandmother. She taught me how to bake."

"She taught us both how to bake and cook, for that matter. We've got her old recipe books. It's lovely to see where she would have written them." Susan was looking around her in wonder.

"History is a wonderful thing, isn't it? Part nostalgia, part memory and part pain. I hope it hasn't been too upsetting for you. We've certainly been very happy here and I get the impression it's been a happy house."

Neither Susan nor I were going to spoil Tony's perceptions of his beloved home, so we nodded and made polite noises.

We passed through the door at the opposite end of the kitchen and were back 'above stairs'. I looked around the lofty hallway and the elegant decorations. There was no denying, it was a beautiful house. Many people would be bitter that their family fortunes had changed so dramatically, but not me. I was glad I'd come, but I would have no sense of what might have been when we left.

"Is there anything else you'd like to ask or know?" Charles led us back into the drawing room.

This was it. I took a deep breath.

"Actually, I was wondering, could I possibly look at the Summer House?"

CHAPTER 36

"The tour around the house has been lovely and it has definitely brought back some memories. But the place I most associate with my time here is the Summer House. I feel it's almost part of my DNA." Well, that wasn't a lie, I thought.

"It's kitted out as my art studio now, so it's a bit of a mess, but you're very welcome to have a look inside. You probably won't remember, but it's just down the driveway then off to the right on a sort of..."

"Stepping stone path." We both finished the sentence, then smiled.

"I'll take you down there, but you can't miss it. And if you carry on past the Summer House, the stepping stones end and a path to the woods begins. It splits in two, one way to the trees, the other to the quarry."

This was the opening I needed.

"I was going to ask about the quarry. Is it possible to get to?"

"Not in those shoes," said Tony looking at our elegant court shoes with dainty heels. "It's a bit rough under foot. You'll definitely need trainers. There's not a lot to see, though."

"Is it accessible by the general public?" Susan asked.

"No, we have the only access. A local housing developer approached us not long after we moved in. He was full of plans for the fields surrounding the quarry, but we are the only place for an access road. We said no—we couldn't have said anything other than no. The woodland and the surrounding patch up to and including the quarry is protected. Your grandfather William put a covenant on the land. It doesn't run out for another forty years or so."

"Really, how interesting." I enthused.

Behind my polite response, my mind was in overdrive. I was more convinced than ever that this was Robert's final resting place. There were simply too many coincidences.

"We've got our trainers in the car. Would you mind if we went to have a look?" I tried my best Monmouth charm.

"Be our guest," said Charles. "If you're not back by sundown, we'll send a search party. Shall we start with the Summer House?"

"I won't come if you don't mind. I've got some research to do. Do pop in before you go, ladies, as I can give you the information I found out about your family."

"That would be wonderful, Tony, thank you."

"Not at all. There's nothing I love more than digging up family skeletons."

Tony's words followed us out of the house, down the steps and to my car. I lifted the boot and took out our alternative footwear.

"Are you ok, Eve?"

"I think so, yes. I got really strong déjà vu at times, but I think I'm glad I came. You?"

"I still can't believe we lived here at all. It seems so far away from Scotland."

"Let's talk later. Charles will be wondering what on earth we're doing."

Shoes replaced, we went to join him. He was standing as if he had all the time in the world. It struck me that he looked like a man who would take most things in his stride. Maybe not a killing in his art studio, though.

As we trod down the stepping stone path, my heart started to race again. This was it. I was about to be confronted with the place where it had all happened. As we rounded a huge rhododendron bush, the Summer House suddenly appeared.

I almost cried with relief. For some silly reason, I'd been expecting a carbon copy of mine. This was a very different beast. For starters, it was much much bigger, and it was a totally different shape. No octagonal base here. It was a squarish oblong structure in well-seasoned wood. It looked like a single storey chalet with a little veranda running around the outside. A small wooden staircase led up to big double doors, which would let in all the light Charles would need for his work.

From the outside, it struck no chords with me. Maybe inside would be a different story. Charles pushed open the doors, which were sticking slightly and ushered us inside. The desk and chaise longue of Doris's description were long gone. The floors were rug free and stripped back to bare boards. Apart from a saggy old chair, a cluttered desk, and a groaning bookcase on the back wall, everything else in the room screamed art. Art in progress, art finished, and art to be started. Three or four easels were stacked with canvasses and pieces of paper. The smell of turpentine was strong but not totally overpowering.

I waited for nostalgia to hit me, but it didn't. How strange that the place I'd loved so much as a child should move me so little. Maybe its transformation had something to do with that. It bore no resemblance to the place Doris and I had spent our afternoons in. I didn't know whether I should be glad or disappointed.

"It's a wonderful spot here. The light is marvellous. Thankfully, it's hooked up to the main house so I can be self-sufficient with coffee and toast."

"It's funny. Now I'm here, I don't seem to remember it at all. I really thought I would. There was a wooden chest that held my toys which was always here. I do have memories of that, but maybe that's because we still have it. It's in the room my great-granddaughter sleeps in when she comes to stay. I'm trying to imagine where it would have stood."

"I can't help with that, but I can show you how the previous owners had it laid out. They used it as a Summer House and had been here for the best part of thirty years. They left all the furniture here and I painted the place as it was as a sort of record before I turned it into my studio. Give me a minute; I'll find it."

Charles approached the groaning bookcase and flicked through various folders. He selected a painting, returned triumphantly and propped it on the nearest easel.

"It's not as it would have been in your day, obviously, but it gives a good idea of how it might have looked. If ever we were to use the place for its original purpose, we'd arrange it something like this."

Susan and I leant forward to inspect the painting. It depicted a room with chairs on either side of a table facing the doors. Huge bookcases lined the back walls. It was a good representation, but it meant nothing to me. The rich furnishings that I'd played amongst were missing and I just couldn't get a sense of how it would have been.

"I really love working in here. There's a great energy, almost like something urges me on to unleash my creativity. I've certainly been very productive in this space. I've another exhibition coming up and that will be the third I've done since moving here."

I was glad Charles found it so energising. I just felt flat.

"Thanks so much for letting us have a look. It must have seemed strange when Susan contacted you out of the blue."

"Not at all. We knew the house must have a history, so it's lovely to meet the people who were part of it."

"It was all so long ago now. But it's been lovely to see it. I think we'll walk up to the quarry now if that's ok?"

"Of course, just call at the house when you are done. Take your time. There's a bit of a walk around the top but be careful, it's not a well-trodden path."

Susan and I assured him we'd be fine and climbed down the steps to the stepping stones. I turned to take another look at the place where my life had quite literally begun. It looked calm and tranquil. Slipping my phone out of my bag, I took a few snaps.

Susan and I set off along the remaining stepping stones to join the path. I felt relieved; there were no ghosts here.

CHAPTER 37

Susan seemed to realise I needed some processing time. She walked alongside me in companionable silence. I could feel her eyes on me every now and then, just checking I was ok. I was glad she was there.

And how was I feeling? Definitely flat. I'd expected to have some kind of reaction to the Summer House. I'd prepared myself for the worst, so to feel nothing at all was unnerving. I felt no connection with the building. I couldn't picture Robert lying there with Doris's shocked face looking down on him. I couldn't imagine the blood on the rug or Mum and Dad arriving on the scene and taking over. I'd built the place up so much in my mind and it had fallen woefully short.

Maybe that was a good thing. Hopefully, this would mean my own little summer house would feel like mine again. On the whole, I had to take this as a positive, didn't I? I emerged from my reflections.

"Sorry, Sue, I was miles away."

"I guessed you would be. Do you want to talk about it?"

"I'm not sure what to tell you. I didn't feel anything. No déjà vu, no emotional intensity, no horror and not even any tears."

"Do you think that matters?"

"I don't know; I suppose I was expecting some kind of epiphany. God knows why."

"Well, I think the fact you didn't react is a good thing. You may change your mind in a day or two, of course. You have to be prepared for that."

"Yes, I've already thought about that. And of course, we haven't been to the quarry yet."

Charles had been right. The path was visible but clearly not used often. Conversation ceased while we picked our way along the narrow and, at times, uneven pathway. The trees thinned out on our left and the expanse of fields came into view. A rise in the ground led us up to the ridge around the edge of the quarry. As expected, the edges dropped, cliff-like in places, down to the murky water below. I shivered. Even on this warm, sunny day, there was something eerie about the place. I wondered how many bodies might have been concealed here over the years. For goodness sake, I was getting fanciful. I shook myself free of such macabre thoughts.

"Gives you the creeps, doesn't it?"

"I'm glad it's not just me." I smiled at my sister in solidarity.

"How do you want to do this? Do you want to walk all the way around first?"

"No, I don't think so. If this is the place, I can't imagine Dad struggling too far to do the deed. Mind you, I can't imagine him doing it at all!"

"No, the thought of it seems like some kind of bizarre fantasy. Are you absolutely sure you want to do this?"

"Yes, whether it's the right place or not, I can at least give Robert a send-off."

It seemed natural to me to follow the edge of the quarry clockwise. The path was even more rugged, and it had clearly been some time since Charles and Tony had ventured this way. We negotiated brambles and nettles, trying to keep our dainty dresses close to for protection. After ten minutes, the path broadened out a little and formed a flattish and mercifully nettle free area. This would do.

I opened my bag and fished out Robert's letter, a small box of matches, the rose and a little bowl. I placed the bowl on the ground and asked Susan to hold the rose and matches.

"I think I should say something, don't you?"

"I'll listen to whatever you say or read, Eve. Just take your time."

Now the moment was here I was a bundle of nerves. I'd never done anything like this before. Susan and I had relied upon the vicar to deliver Mum and Dad's eulogies. I was out of my comfort zone. I closed my eyes and imagined Clive next to me. He'd smile and brush his fingers across my cheeks before telling me I'd do a great job. I straightened my shoulders and cleared my throat.

"Today I'm going to read a letter to a man called Robert Parr. I never met him, yet he is part of me, and I am part of him. I hope these words serve as a fitting tribute to the man who gave me life..."

Dear Robert,

I'm so very sorry I never had the chance to meet you. Your existence was unknown to me until very recently. I have so much to say but an inadequate supply of words to do so.

Your life was snatched away too soon. For that, I apologise on Doris's behalf. I'm sure it's no consolation, but she did regret her actions and she certainly had no intention to harm you. The fact that she took your life has weighed heavily since I found out. But it wasn't only your life that was taken, your memory was taken too, not only by Doris but by my entire family. I apologise for this as well. My family wiped your name from the history books. You have no known final resting place and no fitting send-off for a man who, by all accounts, was good and kind. I have found this hard to come to terms with.

You gave me life. Without you, I wouldn't be here, and for that,

I'm truly grateful. Please know your daughter has had a good life. I have a wonderful husband and family. You have two grandchildren, five great-grandchildren and a great-great-granddaughter. They are your legacy. They are your pages in the history books. Through them, you will not be forgotten. Your name will not be unknown to them. This is my pledge.

Rest well, rest in love and rest in peace.

Love from
Eve X

I could see Susan wiping her eyes with a bowed head. I took a shaky breath. It was amazing how emotional I felt about a man I'd never met. I'd been so unsure about reading the letter aloud, but I was glad I had. With those words, I'd committed myself and it felt right. I tore the letter into pieces and put them into the bowl. Susan handed me the matches, and I fumbled with adrenalin-fuelled fingers. Finally, I managed to strike and light one of the pieces. The flame caught and licked through the bowl, turning the rest of the letter into ash. I let it settle. When it was cool enough to lift, I picked it up and walked towards the edge. Without words, I held out my hand, and Susan placed the rose there.

"To Robert Parr, my father."

I lifted the bowl and shook the ash free. It danced in the air and started to fall. I sent the rose after it and watched as the just-opened petals flirted with air and ash before descending. Susan and I watched it until we could see it no more.

The minutes stood still yet rushed on by and still we were silent.

"Thank you for coming with me," I said eventually.

"I wouldn't have missed it. How do you feel now?"

"Good...I think. I certainly feel calmer. Funnily enough, saying goodbye to a man I never met has made total sense."

"I'm so glad. I know these last few weeks have been unbelievably difficult for you. But you really can't be held accountable for Doris's actions or our parents."

"I know and I can't change their behaviour either. I hate what Doris did to Robert. I hate that Mum and Dad and our grandparents covered it all up. But you're right, I'm not responsible for any of it."

I glanced down at the pink rose pinned to my jacket. Doris had suffered too, of course. A lost love, her upbringing and the times had all combined with her nature and resulted in tragedy. She must have been devastated to leave me behind. I couldn't imagine having to do that to my children. I unpinned the rose and smoothed the velvet petals between my fingers.

"To Doris Monmouth...my mother." She'd always be a Monmouth to me. Her rose arced, then fell and disappeared out of sight. I ran a tissue around the bowl and shook away the last few speckles of ash. It was time to go.

CHAPTER 38

Charles and Tony had insisted we stay for lunch, and we gratefully accepted. We ate in the dining room, the setting for many an emotional scene while Doris had lived here. Storms bigger than any teacups we could imagine had raged around this elegant room.

All was tranquil today and we sat to eat a simple fare of sandwiches and salad. Charles and Tony were the perfect hosts; relaxed, engaging and attentive. The house suited them and they seemed very happy here. I was glad the Monmouth shame hadn't scarred the place. It was in good hands.

Mindful of Tony's afternoon appointment and not wishing to outstay our welcome, we started the farewell rituals.

"Thank you so much for allowing us to come. You've no idea how important it was to us and how much it has meant." I clasped Tony's hand.

"We're delighted you came. Now don't forget the family research. I only gave you a brief outline earlier. There's more in the folder."

I took it from him and turned to Charles.

"Here's two pairs of tickets in case you fancy coming to my next exhibition." Charles kissed both my cheeks before turning to Susan.

"How lovely, thank you." I tucked the tickets into my bag.

As ever, the actual act of saying goodbye and leaving was a protracted affair. Another goodbye on the doorstep followed and then both Charles and Tony accompanied us to the car.

"Actually, do you mind if I take one last photograph of the house?"

"Be our guest. In fact, we'll get one of the two of you in front of your old home, shall we?" Tony was reaching for my phone.

"Better leave that to me, To. You know your eye isn't as good as mine." Charles took possession of my phone and directed Susan and I into the best place for the light.

"I've taken several, just to be on the safe side."

"Could we get one of you two as well? I can't claim to have your eye, Charles, but I'll do my best." Susan smiled and signalled for them to swap places with us.

"Eve, go and stand with Charles and Tony. I'll get one last shot."

One-hundred-watt smiles flashed and the moment was captured.

"We really must be on our way now. Thank you again from the bottom of my heart. I won't forget this." I was starting to feel a bit emotional.

"You can pop in anytime. I know we're not exactly on the passing by route, but you'd be very welcome." Charles took my hand. "We mean it, you know."

And somehow, I knew he was being sincere.

Susan and I took our places in the car. I turned the ignition and we waved out of our respective windows. The tyres swooshed over the gravel and we were on our way.

Once more, at the end of the drive, I stopped the car. Parts of the house were still visible from here and I turned to look back over my shoulder. That was the Monmouth family history. It was also our history and our past. I was glad we'd come, but it was time to move forward. I set the car in motion. Just as Doris must have done on the morning when she tried to take me, I sat at the junction at the end of the drive. I checked for traffic and pulled out. We too, turned left but headed on a different path to Doris.

These Monmouth girls were heading to the future.

CHAPTER 39

The last twenty-four hours had been a bit of a blur. I know we'd enjoyed a delicious meal at the Indian restaurant Edward had booked for us. I also know I'd phoned Clive and attempted to fill him in. In the end, he said he'd wait until I got back.

This morning, I'd spent a little bit of time looking at the folder Tony had given to me. No doubt there were some fascinating and truly shocking facts, but my brain wasn't prepared to absorb them yet. I busied myself looking back through the photos I'd taken at Fremell Hall instead. I was pleased that they hadn't made me feel uneasy or uncomfortable. Maybe it was too early to judge, but so far, I was glad I'd come. Susan had been right. It had helped me to put the past back where it belonged. I was ready to go home and embrace what life had still got to offer.

The car seemed to devour the miles this time. I couldn't wait to get back and see Clive and Benji.

"I'm so grateful, Sue. Thanks for pushing me to do this. I really feel it was the right thing to do."

"Well, I'm glad it's helped. When you had your funny turn in the drawing room, I wondered if I'd made a big mistake."

"I think it was just reaction. It felt strange to be back and feel a kind of connection to a place I haven't lived in for so long. I wasn't expecting it."

"It's a beautiful house, isn't it? It must have been a very different sort of life. I've always wondered what it would be like to live somewhere like that. Now I've seen it up close, though, I know it's not the life for me. I'm content with mine and Duncan's house and our life."

"Me too. I wouldn't swap what I've got for all the tea in China."

"Or all the tea in the family Clipper," joked Susan.

"No wonder we drink so much of the damn stuff. It's hard-wired into our DNA. I'll certainly be ready for a cup when we get back."

I didn't have long to wait. Forty minutes later, I'd dropped Susan off and was pulling onto my familiar and oh so welcome short drive. No gravel, just simple flags, but it was home.

Benji practically knocked me over with his enthusiastic welcome. He tried to lick every available inch of my hands, but I evaded his tongue and gently pushed him away. He hurtled up the corridor, very nearly tripping Clive.

"Hello, love. I won't welcome you quite like Benji, but we've both missed you."

His arms came around me in a welcoming hug, and I pulled him tightly towards me. It felt good to be back.

"I've missed you too. I've got so much to tell you. I know I didn't make much sense last night."

"Not really, no. I've been curbing my curiosity all day. Let's get the kettle on and you can fill me in."

Our kitchen, tiny in comparison to the one in Fremell Hall, was like an oasis. I looked around and drank it all in with a new appreciation. Clive filled the kettle and popped it on the Aga.

"Go and sit in the sunroom. I'll bring everything through."

Just like the kitchen, the sunroom looked as it always did. It was comforting to see our chairs and Benji's bed simply waiting for the occupants to claim them. The chairs really could do with replacing or at least re-covering, but we never seem to get around to it. The coffee table held today's paper with the crossword uppermost. I wondered if Clive had finished it yet.

Inevitably, my eye was drawn to the garden and the Summer House. There it sat in all its pretty pale green glory. It was time to lay this ghost to rest. I opened the door that led onto the garden and crossed the grass. I hesitated by the door. Leaning forward, I peered inside.

"Come on, Eve! Just go in!" I muttered to myself.

I pressed the handle down and the door swung inwards. My feet went into autopilot and carried me across the threshold. And just like that, I was in. I gave myself a minute to take an objective look around. Two wicker chairs with somewhat lumpy cushions, one wicker and glass table, a heater and another table against one wall, which we used to stash booze and mixers on when we were making a night of it.

This little place had played host to many happy memories. Here I'd read stories to Rob and Marianne and then to our grandchildren and great-grandchild. Clive and I had entertained friends and family out here. We'd stargazed, sat in companionable silence and listened to our favourite music. On the odd occasion, we'd even had a dance in it. It was full of love, laughter and memories. My memories, not Doris's. It was my life story encased in these walls, not hers.

"Eve?"

I stepped back into the garden.

"Out here, love. Bring the tea."

Clive made his way cautiously across the grass. His hands really were starting to struggle with arthritis now. I met him halfway and relieved him of the mugs. I set them on the table, and we eased ourselves into the chairs with a little sigh.

"I was being foolish, wasn't I?"

"Well, maybe a little, but you'd had a shock."

"It's nothing like the Summer House at Fremell Hall, you know. It couldn't be more different. The whole trip was such an eye-opener, Clive. I'm so glad I went."

"So, tell me all about it then."

***

The tea mugs sat cold and empty. I'd told Clive everything and shown him the photographs, and he'd briefly flicked through Tony's folder of information.

"I kept a copy of the letter to Robert."

"I did wonder about that."

"I've decided I need to tell the children. They should know their family history. I promised Robert I wouldn't let his name be forgotten."

"Eve, you know I'll support your decision, but have you thought this through?"

"Yes. We can't shy away from the less than savoury actions of our ancestors. We can only do our best to be good and decent people in our own lifetimes. Tony is living proof. He's bought a beautiful house which was funded in part by a practice that may have contributed to the death of some of his ancestors. He was the one who said history is part nostalgia and part pain and he's right."

"Well, I can't argue with that. The history books are littered with the terrible actions of humans."

"Exactly, we can't be held responsible, but we can't pretend it didn't happen either. I just think it's so important that they know. It's not like Doris and her story are going to be headline news. Our faces won't adorn the gossip magazines. We don't have to tell anyone outside the family circle. But and this is crucial, Robert won't have been forgotten. His life won't have been for nothing."

"What about his family, Eve? He could have great-nieces and nephews trying to discover what happened to him. Will you seek them out too? Just be careful before you prise the lid off the can of worms."

"You've forgotten, Clive, his family, well his immediate family, were already dead when he met Doris. The Blitz, remember?"

"Yes, I had forgotten that. Well, it sounds as if you've made your mind up."

"I guess I have. I'll invite Rob and Marianne around for Sunday lunch. Any kind of revelation is best served with food."

CHAPTER 40

The family revelations had gone surprisingly well. Of course, there had been shock and disbelief. Neither Rob nor Marianne could imagine their grandparents in the roles they had been told of. To be fair, it was still something I struggled with too.

In a way, Rob almost seemed relieved. Doris's behaviour, though shocking, had actually given him a line in the sand that he never wanted to cross. This seemed to give him comfort. He still took responsibility for his own anger-fuelled actions, but now at least, he understood the real tragedy it could lead to. Hearing about Doris and, of course, my own temper had helped him to make sense of himself is how he described it to me as he carried the dirty dishes through to the kitchen. That was certainly an aspect of this situation I hadn't thought about.

He and his sister were both agog to see the letters and the folder. In the end, eldest child's rights won out. Rob left with them and promised to pass them to Marianne as soon as he'd finished. Marianne had inherited her Aunt Susan's rampant curiosity, so there was no way he'd be allowed to hang onto them indefinitely.

As for Rob and Marianne's mostly grown-up children, they were going to decide how and when they should be told. I'd reassured them I'd be there to break the news whenever that was. Funnily enough, the more times I told the tale, the easier it became. I guess familiarity brings a certain amount of laissez-faire to the proceedings.

The only thing I hadn't done anything about was Noel and Charlotte. As the family on this side of the world healed and grew into their new history, those on the other side were still none the wiser. Weeks then months had slipped by. The seasons had changed, and a New Year welcomed in, and still, their contact details lay beside my bed. Twice, I'd opened my email and started to type their addresses. Twice something had stopped me from progressing further. I knew I had to do something. They must know that I'd have received Doris's letters by now. Surely they'd be waiting to see if this long-lost half-sister was going to get in touch.

The way I saw it, I had three choices. One, simply do nothing. Ignore the contact details, pretend they didn't exist and move on. I'd dismissed this option some time ago. That left the other two choices. I could make contact and establish communication and eventually tell them the truth. Or I could make contact and never mention the darker side of Doris's life.

Until this whole situation with the letters, I'd always been a bit of a ditherer. Clive had spent hours listening while I discussed minute details about various life choices over the years. The visit to Fremell Hall seemed to have kick-started a new dynamism. I was still talking things over with Clive, but my decisions were more or less in place by the time I did this. The issue of Noel and Charlotte was the only thing I was still unsure of.

The phone rang and I picked it up.

"Hi, it's only me."

"Hi, Sue, how are you?"

"Good, but that's not why I called. Guess what dropped through the letterbox the morning?"

"I'm not sure I want to know after the last few months."

"Don't be daft. It's nothing awful. It was the new holiday brochure. I've been flicking through, and there's an organised trip taking in Sydney, Melbourne, Adelaide and Perth and of course, it got me thinking."

"Thinking what?" Susan's 'just thinkings' were legendary in the family.

"Well, it looks fantastic, obviously, but more importantly, you could come with us and get in touch with Noel and Charlotte in Perth. That's where they live, isn't it?"

"Yes, but steady on, Sue. I've not even made contact yet."

"Maybe this is a sign that you should. Why don't you get in touch with them, Eve, and then next year you could actually meet them?" Susan's enthusiasm was carrying her away.

"Easy, tiger, it all sounds a bit fast. They might not want to meet me. We have no idea how they feel about their long-lost half-sister. Besides, I still haven't fully thought about how to get in touch and what on earth I'll say."

"Stop thinking about it, just do it. Look, none of us are getting any younger and who knows what the next year or so will bring. You know Duncan and I have always wanted to go Down Under. We could all go together. It would be so much fun."

"I'm not promising anything regarding the trip at the moment, but I will contact Noel and Charlotte. I'm still trying to work out how much to tell them."

"The bare minimum," said Susan promptly. "Get in touch, establish communication, get to know them and then decide. You can't just say 'Hi, I'm the sister you didn't know about and by the way, our mother was a killer.' It will stop the conversation in its tracks."

Susan always had a way of making her point. Hearing her say it so bluntly made me realise she was right. I couldn't disrupt these people's lives with such dramatic revelations in one go. It would be too much.

"I know, I know, you're right. I'll make contact and let fate take care of itself."

"And don't forget about the trip. Mention it to Clive."

"Will do, I promise."

I took myself off to the study armed with the inevitable mug of tea. I sat down, opened up my email and stared at it. The screen stared uncompromisingly back at me. It was daring me to write but where the hell to begin? I took the coward's way out and went through my inbox instead.

There was one from the local garden centre, which proved a welcome distraction. I flicked through their special offers making a mental note of some of the plants and shrubs. As I scrolled through the newsletter, the 'new stock' section caught my eye.

Just Robert Roses –
available to order for the Robert or Rob in your life.

Surely this had to be a sign. I clicked on the photograph and a beautiful bloom enlarged on the screen. It was a pale pink colour with quite tightly packed petals. It looked fuller than the more common varieties of rose, and the petals were small and less rose-like. It would be a lovely way to mark Robert's life. I didn't need to think about it. I simply placed the order and received confirmation that my Just Robert would be delivered in three days' time.

The rest of my inbox was junk or things that could be attended to or indeed forgotten about until another time. I couldn't put off my real task any longer.

I took a sip of tea, added Noel and Charlotte's email addresses and started to type.

CHAPTER 41

It was time. Clive had nipped out to collect a parcel, Benji was asleep in his bed, and I had a job to do. I pottered around making sure I had everything I needed. I slipped on my gardening shoes and went to the shed to retrieve my trowel and hand fork from their little hooks. The half bag of compost was next. That was harder work than I expected, and I had to sit in the Summer House for a few minutes to get over the exertion. Once I'd recovered, I nipped into the house to collect my gardening gloves and kneeling mat. I threw them onto the grass and returned to the house for some old newspaper which joined the collection of tools for the job in hand. Finally, I turned to the black pot sitting by the back door. All I had to do was carry the Just Robert out to its new home.

True to form, Benji woke from his sleep and pranced around my feet in the most unhelpful way imaginable. I kicked his ball across the grass and, while he was distracted, managed to carry the plant from the back door without mishap. We'd had raised beds put in either side of the Summer House doors about ten years after it was built. It seemed the ideal spot for the rose. I glanced around and made sure everything I needed was in easy reach.

Benji returned with his ball but seemed to realise I wasn't in the mood for playing. He flopped down in the middle of the lawn and left me in peace. The soil in the bed was fairly malleable and came out easily enough. I dug and tipped trowel loads of it onto the newspaper on the ground. It was quite hypnotic. Once I was satisfied that the hole was big enough, I picked up the plant.

With a gentle tap on the base of the plastic pot and a bit of shake, the rose plant slid free. I lowered it into the hole and started to scoop the soil back in. I pressed it down with my fingers in between the final scoops until I was satisfied that it seemed stable enough.

With a bit of a groan, I levered myself up and fished the watering can out of the shed. It was a bright pink flamingo that one of the grandchildren had given me. It always made me smile. I filled it at the outside tap and returned to the Just Robert.

I watched as the water poured out of the spout. Droplets bounced off the leaves and down to the soil. It must have been very thirsty as the liquid was absorbed immediately. The water continued to fall, and the plant drank gratefully. It would flourish in this spot; I'd make sure of it. Can empty, I stood back content.

"There you go, Robert Parr. Welcome to your new home. You won't be forgotten here."

Benji stretched and came over to sniff before padding back inside. Anything above his own watering height was of little interest to him. I tidied up the tools and the compost and carried the kneeling mat, gloves and newspaper back inside.

Clive must be back as there was a pile of brown paper and an empty cardboard box and bubble wrap on the side.

"Tea?" he asked as he came into the kitchen.

"What's the parcel then?"

"I'll tell you over a brew and a biscuit. Summer House or sunroom?"

"Summer House; I can show you Just Robert."

"You head on out. I'll bring the tray."

As I crossed the garden, it struck me how beautiful the pink rose would look when it bloomed against the pale green wood. I gave the leaves a gentle caress as I passed by. The Summer House had never looked so inviting. I went in and sat in my chair with an air of contentment.

"I thought we'd have a pot," announced Clive.

He deposited the tray on the table and started to dish out the cups and saucers. Cups and saucers? And the milk jug and sugar bowl had come out as well. He'd even dug a tea cosy out, which was smothering a teapot in woolly warmth.

"What's the occasion?"

Clive lifted the tea cosy with a flourish. The 'Forget-me-not' teapot sat in front of me. The cracks had been filled with gold which matched the original rim colour, and the pot was whole again. I gasped and ran my fingers over the newly mended surface—it was beautiful.

Each crack looked as though it were meant to be there, as if it were somehow part of the artistry. I turned it around, careful not to slosh any tea out of the spout. The repair work actually elevated the teapot. No longer was it one of hundreds that had been mass-produced, now it was totally unique. Its beauty was its difference. The glorious flaws were highlighted and celebrated. I was overwhelmed.

"Thank you, Clive. It's beautiful, just beautiful."

He smiled at me and lifted my hand to his lips.

"Shall we see if it still pours?"

The tea came gushing out without spilling a drop. In appearance and function, it was imperfectly perfect. I loved it. No longer would this teapot sit unused in a display cabinet. It would not be kept for 'special occasions'. Everyday life and living were special occasions. From now on, it would be used for our many cups of teas and serve as a reminder that my life was also imperfectly perfect.

ACKNOWLEDGEMENTS

People often say that writing is a lonely business. Although the actual putting pen to paper can be, the people involved in making the book a reality ensure you never feel totally alone.

There are many to thank, starting with the fabulous team at TAUK Publishing. Sue Miller and Estelle Maher have held my nervous hands as I transitioned from children's author to short story creator and now to fully-fledged novelist. It's been a totally different experience and they have offered their support, expertise and friendship throughout. The book would not be here without them.

Enormous thanks to Michelle Catanach, who has created the beautiful cover for the book. It's absolutely perfect.

Thanks also to my writing support group 'Frank and Friendly', which is made up of fellow writers Jenny Jones, Stephanie Power and Lesley Rawlinson. They have been in it for the long haul, pointing out plot holes, making sure my characters were clearly defined and helping me question and develop my writing. Kintsugi would not be the novel it is without them. The lunches in various establishments along Lark Lane also helped!

Huge thanks to my BETA readers Cath Burrows, Ali Gill, Luisa A Jones, Bob Stone and Maddy Templeman, who took the time to read the novel. Their feedback and encouragement was invaluable. Bob gets an extra mention as he cast a wise book seller's eye over my blurb and helped to tighten it up.

Special thanks to my dad and Lenny, my brother, who always read my work and provide encouragement. As for my partner Dom, his encouragement is beyond measure. He is unfailingly supportive of all my creative endeavours and can always be relied upon to offer wise words, chocolate, and cups of tea, although not served in a teapot like Eve's.

Finally, I thank you. Thank you for picking up my book. Maybe you were drawn to it by the fabulous cover. Perhaps the blurb intrigued you and you decided to flick through the pages and take a chance on it. Maybe you inhaled the aroma of the paper, there's no shame in that. I do it too. However my book came into your life, I thank you for reading and hopefully enjoying it.

If you could take a minute to review the book on Amazon, Goodreads or my Facebook page, I'd be extremely grateful.

Follow me on:

Facebook.com/JudeLennonAuthor

Twitter.com/JudeLennonBooks

Instagram.com/JudeLennonBooks

ABOUT THE AUTHOR

Jude Lennon is a former Early Years teacher who escaped the chalk face and set up a storytelling business called Little Lamb Tales. When she isn't telling stories at primary schools, community events, festivals and libraries, Jude loves to write. She has published around twenty children's picture books and chapter books. Many of them feature her storytelling mascots, Lamby and Flossie. In 2019, Jude published a collection of short stories for adults, which set her on the path to writing her first full-length novel.

Jude is passionate about books, words, stories and creativity and believes that reading is the door to the world. When she isn't writing or reading, she loves walking, dancing or camping in her vintage van, Buttercup. She's also rather partial to chocolate and gin. Sometimes even at the same time!

Jude lives in Liverpool with her partner Dom who is a musician. She has become adept at blocking out the sound of drums while writing.

You can find out more about Jude at:

www.littlelambpublishing.co.uk